THE VAMPIRE WAR

DARK WORLD: THE VAMPIRE WISH 5

MICHELLE MADOW

DREAMSCAPE PUBLISHING

ANNIKA

ICY WATER RUSHED at my feet, and I gasped at the contact, my eyes snapping open.

The sun barely peaked through the dark clouds above, and the water around me was tinted red with blood. With *my* blood.

I'd lost more blood than should be humanly possible. But I couldn't worry about myself right now. Instead, I searched for Jacen.

He was where I remembered—passed out on the other side of the boat. The water hadn't reached him yet. At least I *hoped* he was passed out.

The sea creature couldn't have killed him, could it have? Jacen was a powerful vampire prince—rumored to be one of the strongest vampires ever turned. He couldn't be gone.

I couldn't live with myself if he were. He'd jumped in front of that monster to save me. And he was only here because I'd invited him on this quest.

The quest was supposedly my destiny to complete.

Surely destiny couldn't be so cruel as to bring Jacen and me together again only to rip him from me right when it might be possible for us to finally be together?

I rushed to him, ignoring the pain that pounded through my head with every step. I'd been injured too—the sea creature had shredded my wrist when I'd thrown the stake up through the roof of its mouth to kill it—but I had to fight through the wooziness.

I had to verify that Jacen was alive.

I kneeled down next to him, my tears landing on his chest as I cupped a hand around his cheek. His skin was paler than usual—too pale, even for a vampire—and he didn't open his eyes at my touch. But he was breathing. That was a good start.

His legs had been mangled when the sea creature caught him in its jaws. They were covered in blood, but his bones were moving themselves back into place, his muscles and skin weaving back together. The healing was slow—I suspected because he'd lost so much blood —but at least he was healing.

He was going to be okay.

And for the first time since rushing over to him, I realized that my own hand was healing as well.

It must be because of my Nephilim abilities. I was still coming to terms with the fact that I was Nephilim—possibly the last Nephilim on the planet—and I still didn't know the extent of my abilities. But as far as abilities went, healing seemed like a useful one to have. Especially since supernaturals couldn't drink vampire blood—which had healing abilities—without getting sick. The only people who could drink vampire blood for its healing properties were humans.

Now that I knew that both Jacen and I were recovering from our injuries, I looked out to the giant tree glowing on an island in the distance. It wasn't just any old tree.

It was the Tree of Life.

The sight of the majestic Tree *should* have brought me peace. But while I was no sea captain, it seemed like at the rate that the water was flowing into the boat, we had no chance of making it to the island before sinking.

"Jacen." I returned my hand to his face again. "Wake up."

He didn't wake.

Even if he *did* wake, what would we do? His legs still weren't even halfway healed. Despite his having been a champion swimmer back when he'd been human, he was in no shape to swim to the island. And my strength still hadn't fully returned.

How could I get the two of us to land safely?

A solution came to me quickly. When the boat's engine had first stopped working, I'd gone into the supply room and grabbed two paddles—the paddles I'd eventually stuffed into the sea monster's nostrils to force it to open its mouth and let Jacen free.

There'd been life preservers next to the paddles.

I didn't want to leave Jacen's side, but I forced myself away from him. Saving our lives was the most useful thing I could do right now.

I ran to the supply room and swung the door open, my eyes widening as I looked down the steps. The room was nearly filled with water.

Most of the objects inside appeared to be destroyed. But a few bright orange life vests floated on the other side.

I swam over to them, my head nearly brushing against the ceiling with each stroke. The icy water made my teeth chatter uncontrollably. But I kept moving, since moving would keep me from freezing to death.

It felt like it took forever, but I eventually reached the life vests. I laid one arm on top of one and the other on top of the second. The water was rising quickly—I had to angle my head upward to give myself room to breathe. I needed to get out of there. So I used my feet to push off from the wall and shoot straight to the other side like a torpedo. Once there, I pulled myself and the life vests out of the room.

Seconds after I was out of there, more water rushed through, filling the room completely.

I hurried back over to Jacen, somehow managing to get the life preserver on his unconscious body. Once making sure it was secure, I put mine on myself.

Suddenly, silver glinted off to the side—my sword. It had been thrust from my hand while I'd been fighting the sea creature, which was why I'd had to kill the monster by throwing my stake. But my stake was gone, and I needed a weapon. So I ran to the sword, taking it and shoving it into the sheath that was still attached to my back. I wasn't sure if the life vest would keep both me and the sword afloat, or if I'd be able to swim with the sword at all, but didn't want to risk reaching the island and not having a way to protect myself.

And so, I ran back over to Jacen, taking his hands in mine and praying to the angels as the water filled the boat, crashing over the deck and consuming it entirely.

ANNIKA

THE PULL of the sinking boat yanked both of us under. The currents tried to rip us apart, but I tightened my grip around Jacen's hands, holding on as hard as I could.

I couldn't lose him. I *refused* to lose him.

I was so turned around that I didn't know which way was up, but the life vests pulled both of us back to the surface. Once there, I sucked in a deep breath, the icy air sharp as it filled my lungs.

I checked Jacen—he was still unconscious, but breathing. Thank God. I didn't know what I would have done otherwise.

I swam to the shore, hauling Jacen and the sword along with me. As I swam, I stayed focused on the Tree. But the icy water was sapping my energy quickly.

To keep myself going, I reminded myself what the

vampire seer Rosella had told me before sending me on this journey. According to Rosella, a dark force—darker than anything the world had seen in centuries—was coming. I, the only known Nephilim on the entire planet, was prophesied to retrieve the Grail from where it had been hidden inside the Tree of Life to stop this force.

I'd been shocked—I hadn't thought the Holy Grail had *existed* until then—but I trusted the seer. Then she'd had another vision and wrote down the coordinates to the three mages. She'd told me that I could select only one person to bring with me on my quest. Select the wrong person, and I'd die. Select the right one, and I'd live.

I knew in my heart that Jacen was the correct choice. I trusted him with my life, and after this, I assumed he would trust me with his. We *weren't* going to sink into an icy grave together. We'd been through too much to have it end like that.

And so I paddled on, relief coursing through my veins as I pulled both Jacen and myself onto shore and collapsed into the warm, dry sand.

ANNIKA

I woke to warm, strong arms encircling me.

"Jacen?" I whispered his name, glancing up at him.

"Hey." His voice was weak, but he managed a smile. "How do you feel?"

"I feel…" I paused, taking a moment to fully assess myself before answering. Given all the blood that I'd lost—and the fact that I'd swam through water in the arctic—I should have been dead.

No—a *human* should have been dead.

But I wasn't a human.

I was Nephilim.

Neither of us were wearing our life vests anymore—he must have removed mine while I'd been sleeping. But he'd left my sword in the sheath on my back.

With Jacen's arms around me and my sword strapped on my back, I felt safer than ever.

"I feel good," I answered honestly. "Great, even. How long was I asleep?"

"A few hours," he said.

"You've been up this whole time?" I gazed up at him, annoyed that he hadn't woken me sooner. Waking naturally in his arms had been amazing—heavenly, even—but we had a quest to accomplish.

"Only for about ten minutes," he said. "You were sleeping so peacefully that I wanted to give you a bit more time to rest."

"Now isn't the time to rest," I reminded him. "We have to get the Grail." I stood up and brushed sand off my clothes, realizing for the first time that they were no longer sopping wet. In fact, even though it was nighttime and we were in the arctic, the island itself was the perfect temperature.

"We do," he agreed. "But first we need to find out if there are any animals on this island."

"Why?" I asked. "Do you think they'll be dangerous?"

"I have no idea," he said. "But dangerous or not, they'll have blood."

I glanced down at his healed legs, remembering all the blood he'd lost earlier. "You need blood," I realized. "And your supply drowned with the boat."

"Yes." He nodded. "But there are tons of shed antlers past the beach. And where there are antlers, there are stags."

I looked to where the beach met the grass, seeing the antlers he was talking about. There were *tons* of them.

But they would hardly solve his problem.

I sat back down, realizing why he still wasn't standing—he couldn't afford to squander any more energy than necessary.

"Animal blood won't give you your full strength back," I said, since I'd learned as much when I'd lived in the Vale. "It'll only give you half the strength as human blood would."

"Half strength is better than nothing," he said. "The vampires at the Haven survive on animal blood, and they're just fine."

"Because tiger shifters protect them."

He opened his mouth to argue, but I continued before he could.

"We don't know what we'll find on this island," I said. "We might need to fight another monster, or we might not." I hoped not, given how our fight with the sea crea-ture had turned out, but I didn't want to say it and jinx us. "You should be at your full strength regardless."

"I'm strong," he reminded me. "The strength I'll gain from the animal blood will be enough."

"It won't be as much as you would get from human blood." I jutted my chin out stubbornly. "We need to be ready for anything."

"So what are you suggesting?" he asked.

"Drink from me," I said simply.

"But you're not human." He pulled back, narrowing his eyes. "You're Nephilim."

"When I appeared in the Haven, the vampires there were overcome with bloodlust." I leaned forward, as if daring him to challenge me. "I assumed that meant that I smelled the same to them as a human."

"You don't," he said.

"Oh." I tilted my head, looking at him thoughtfully. "Does my blood smell *better* than human blood?"

If it did, it meant Jacen was fighting his instinct to feed from me even more than I'd realized—especially now that he was thirsty.

"It does," he confirmed.

Despite the scent of my blood being clearly out of my control, I felt guilty for unknowingly tempting him. But I pushed the guilt aside. Because he needed my blood to be at full strength, so the temptation would be an advantage to me right now.

"Usually supernatural blood is only slightly more appealing than animal blood, which means it's not tempting at all," he said. "That's how vampires at the

Haven live with witches and shifters without the urge to feed from them. But your blood…" He trailed off and pressed his lips together, as if hesitant to continue.

"What about my blood?" I crawled closer, wanting him to think about it. For him to *want* it.

His eyes dilated at how close I was, but he didn't move away. "It smells sweeter and purer than a human's ever could," he murmured, his eyes traveling to my neck with so much precision that I could practically feel it.

"My blood will give you strength." My breathing slowed under the intensity of his gaze. "Drink. Your being at full strength could save both of our lives."

"Or I could kill you." He backed away, shaking his head as if pulling himself out of a daze.

"You won't."

"You don't know that," he said. "You only met me once I'd gotten control of my bloodlust. Before, when I was newly turned…"

"You lost control, went on a rampage, and killed dozens of humans in the Vale," I said bluntly. "I know this. But I also know *you*. You threw yourself into the jaws of a sea monster to save me. You didn't risk your life back there to just kill me now."

"I've never tasted Nephilim blood before." His gaze was hot as he looked down at me. "Neither of us know what will happen if I do."

"You'll be able to stop yourself from killing me." I spoke strongly, as if that could force him to believe me. "Yes, trying might be dangerous. But if you drink animal blood instead, you won't be at full strength, which could put us both in danger. How do you think that fight with the sea monster would have gone if you'd only had animal blood beforehand instead of human blood?"

"You would have fought it off yourself," he said after a short pause. "You're strong, Annika. Stronger than you even realize."

My lips parted—his belief in me had caught me off guard—but I forced myself to focus. "I needed your help in that fight," I said. "I needed your help at *full* strength. Without you, we both would have died, and you know it."

He said nothing, which I assumed meant he agreed with me.

"I'd drain some of my blood into a cup for you, but we lost our dishware with the boat." I pulled my hair away from my neck, leaning closer to him. "So we're going to have to do this the old fashioned way."

He ran a finger slowly down my cheek, his eyes not leaving mine. Then he leaned forward and pressed his lips to mine.

It hadn't been where I'd expected them to go, but I sunk into his kiss anyway.

When he pulled away, his eyes were fierce with desire—and with determination. "If I kill you, I'll never be able to live with myself," he said. "I'll take one of those antlers and drive it straight through my heart."

"No you won't." I took his hand and squeezed it with mine. "Because you won't kill me. I trust you, Jacen. Plus, I'm a Nephilim now. I'm strong. If you take too much, I'm pretty sure I can fight you off." I smiled, although he was too solemn to return it.

He simply nodded before pressing his lips to mine again. But instead of deepening the kiss like he had last time, he trailed the kisses down my chin, all the way down to my neck.

He lingered there for a few seconds, and then I gasped as his fangs pierced my skin.

4

KARINA

I SAT in one of the hard chairs at the Dublin airport, waiting for my flight back to Canada to board. There had been no more first class seats left on the plane, and compelling the airline attendant to bump someone out of first class so I could take their place would cause too much of a scene, so I was stuck in coach—again.

But it didn't matter. All that mattered was getting back to the Vale so I could tell Noah how I felt about him.

It was unheard of for a vampire to feel this way about a shifter, but I didn't care. Because the entire time I'd been a vampire, I'd been empty and floundering. Noah was the first person who made me feel grounded and alive. He was my anchor.

He deserved to know that.

Hopefully he could also tell me why I'd gone to the fae. I couldn't remember, which made me think I must have made a deal with the fae that involved them tampering with my memories. Perhaps it had been something to foster peace between the wolves and the vampires of the Vale? After all, I didn't want the vampires—my own species—to die. But I also understood why the wolves wanted them gone. The wolves had suffered centuries of poverty and war amongst their packs, and their Savior was finally ready to rise. He'd given many wolves visions of his upcoming arrival.

But there was a catch with His rising—it could only happen if there were no more vampires left in the Vale. But centuries ago, the wolves had signed away the portion of their land in a peace treaty with the vampires. So if the wolves wanted their land back, it meant declaring war by breaking the treaty.

Given the promises of their Savior, they were preparing to do just that.

It was one massive mess, and I had no idea who was right and who was wrong anymore. All I knew was that I couldn't wait to return to Noah so he could help me work through exactly what had happened with the fae.

In the meantime, I was too anxious to focus on

reading a book while I waited for the plane, so I stared at the television ahead.

"In a unique development, a man has been arrested after biting multiple people in a public park overnight," the generically pretty blonde newscaster announced. "He ran from the scene of the crime, but several onlookers caught pictures of him on their phones, so he was later found and detained. He claims to be a vampire from the 1920s who believes he's wrongly ended up 'in the future.' He's demanding to be taken to Romania to speak with a 'King Nicolae' to sort everything out. We'll keep you updated with an official picture of the man on the hour."

The story, of course, caught my attention. It was the sort of thing that happened sometimes—a rogue vampire getting loose, losing control of their bloodlust, and attacking humans publicly. Non-royal vampires didn't have the ability of compulsion, so they had to be extremely cautious when they fed. It was why the kingdoms were created in the first place, and why all vampires were required to have an allegiance to a kingdom—to keep them in line.

Whoever this vampire was, his mention of King Nicolae made it likely that he was from the Carpathian Kingdom.

As always when something like this happened, the royal vampires would band together, travel to the location of the incident, compel those who'd been directly impacted by the vampire, and do what they needed to do to keep the vampire in line. Unlike the Vale, the Carpathian Kingdom didn't kill rogue vampires like this on the spot. They were held to fair trials and sentences. Sometimes that meant a stake to the heart, sometimes not.

The human world would go on as normal, using logic to brush off the incident and move on with their lives.

As a royal vampire, I normally helped compel away memories from witnesses. But not this time. Because with Laila dead, I would no longer be welcome in the Carpathian Kingdom.

I'd been sent to the Vale in the first place because King Nicolae had wanted me to work with the wolves to help the Vale fall. He'd been obsessed with Queen Laila for centuries, and this was part of his "great plan" to make Laila lose her kingdom and come crawling straight into his arms.

I knew King Nicolae, and because of that, I knew he would blame me for her death. I couldn't risk returning there.

I was going to the one place where I felt safe—to the Vale, and more importantly, to Noah.

Once my boarding group was called, I gathered my belongings and got in line for the plane, not looking back as the newscaster broadcasted the picture of the rogue vampire.

5

CAMELIA

I woke before sunset to remove my stash of wormwood from its spelled hiding spot and take a swig.

Soon after Prince Scott had declared himself acting king of the Vale, he'd forbidden the few witches that lived here to wear the wormwood stones around our necks that we *always* wore for protection. Wearing wormwood made us immune to vampire compulsion, and being allowed to wear it was a way the vampires showed that they trusted us as equals.

I'd done as Scott had commanded and had handed my amulet over to him. What he *didn't* know was that I'd been taking a dose of wormwood each morning as an extra precaution. The spell around my stash stopped anyone from stumbling upon it, and once the wormwood was in my system, the vampires couldn't smell it.

If they tried to compel me, I'd have to pretend to be affected, but I wanted all the control I could get. Because there was no *way* I was going to let Scott become king.

Which meant that on the next full moon, I needed to go to the fae and bargain with them to become an original vampire.

But first the Vale needed Geneva's sapphire ring. Because if I became an original vampire, I would no longer have my magic. Which meant the Vale would need another witch to hold up the boundary. Geneva was the best for the job, since she was the strongest witch in the world.

It was the perfect plan... except for one major problem.

There was a chance I'd gotten pregnant during my previous encounter with the fae.

I'd gone to the fae to ask how to find Geneva's sapphire ring, and was met by a fae by the name of Prince Devyn. He was willing to answer my question—for a price, of course.

That price had been my virginity.

On top of that, another bargain is also necessary *before* striking a deal with the fae, simply to pay them for crossing over to Earth from their home in the Otherworld. For that payment, I'd promised Prince Devyn my first-born child once he or she came of age.

I thought I'd been so smart in that promise, since I intended to become a vampire, which meant I'd never be able to *have* children.

I supposed it had been arrogant of me to think I could manipulate the fae so easily.

That arrogance had cost me. Because while it was still too early to prove, I couldn't shake the feeling that I was pregnant.

I'd created a potion to get rid of the baby. But I'd hidden it away, unable to drink it. Because the more powerful a witch is, the more difficult it is to get pregnant. I also had no more blood family left in the world.

I wanted to keep this baby.

Yes, the child was promised to the fae. But Prince Devyn only wanted the child once he or she "came of age." Which meant I had *years* to find a solution to that problem.

Right now, I needed to make sure the vampires still thought I was able to become an original vampire.

Because if they knew the truth—that I couldn't become an original vampire until after this baby was born—Scott would officially declare himself king, and who knew how far he would go in his twisted efforts to protect the Vale from the wolves.

6

CAMELIA

I GATHERED in the meeting room with Prince Scott, Prince Alexander, Princess Stephenie, and a few vampire guards.

"We've located the wolves' camp," Scott began. "Hopefully you're pleased that my brother convinced me to send vampire guards for this task instead of civilians." He directed the final part of the commentary to me.

"I am." I nodded, wondering what Alexander had said to his brother to convince him to come to his senses. But we had no time to discuss that right now, so I turned to the guards and asked, "What did you find?"

"Their numbers are greater than we'd previously imagined, and they're preparing for an attack," the head guard, Thomas, spoke. "We're outnumbered. Even with all our guards ready to defend our land, we don't have enough trained fighters to beat them."

"So you're suggesting what?" Scott snarled, banging his fist against the table. "That we give up?"

"Perhaps we should try talking to them." Alexander's voice was soft compared to his brother's. "See what they want, and ask why they've chosen now to break the treaty."

Scott threw his head back and laughed. "The wolves are animals," he said after regaining control of himself. "Yes, centuries ago they were able to come to agreements regarding the terms of the treaty. But we all know that as the years passed, they've lost themselves to their animalistic sides. We saw it when they attacked the town and killed innocent vampires. We can't *bargain* with animals. There's only one way to deal with them— we have to slaughter them."

"Didn't you hear what the guards said?" Alexander asked. "We don't have the numbers. We couldn't slaughter them even if we wanted to."

"So we'll attack them before they can attack us," Scott said. "We'll catch them off guard."

Stephenie cleared throat, and everyone in the room looked to her. "How do you suppose we'll do that?" she asked. "If we don't have the numbers, we don't have the numbers. It doesn't matter if they attack first or we attack first—if there's a war, they'll kill us."

Scott rolled his eyes at her and turned toward the vampire guards. "You're to tell no one what we know about the wolves and their camp." From the way their faces all went slack, I could tell he was compelling them. "Understood?"

"Yes," they said in unison.

"Good." He gave them a wave of his hand. "Now leave us. We have important business to discuss."

The guards emptied the room, leaving me alone with the princes and princess.

"Once we control Geneva, we'll be able to beat the wolves," Scott said smugly. "Unfortunately, it's been some time since we've heard from our third brother."

"He betrayed us." Stephenie rolled her eyes. "I told you not to trust him from the start. He's in love with that girl. Annika." Disdain dripped from her voice when she said the Nephilim's name.

"Shut up!" Scott slammed his fist onto the table again. "There's no way our brother is in love with a filthy Nephilim. He barely knew the girl. Plus, his cell phone has a tracker in it, and I can confirm that it's still at the Haven."

"Perhaps Camelia can do a tracking spell?" Alexander suggested. "Just to be sure."

"The Haven is protected with powerful magic," I said. "A tracking spell can't locate anyone within its boundaries."

"Have you tried?" he asked.

"I have." I held his gaze, since of *course* I'd tried to track the prince. "He's untraceable."

"Good." Scott nodded. "It's further proof that he's in the Haven. We have no reason to think he would have betrayed us. Especially since he made a blood oath to me before leaving."

"Perhaps." Alexander scratched his jaw. "But we should have a backup plan in case he's unable to get the ring."

"We *will* get that ring," Scott said. "In the meantime, we'll try to be patient. Once our brother feels like he can securely call, he will."

"And if he doesn't?" Stephenie asked.

"Simple." Scott smirked. "Then we'll go to the Haven, find him, get the ring, and kill the girl ourselves."

7

JACEN

ANNIKA'S BLOOD was the sweetest I'd ever tasted. After only a few sips, my full strength had returned. It was like the fight with the sea creature had never happened.

I wanted to continue to drink—to relish in the sweetness of her blood—but this was *Annika*. I cared about her. I'd never been in love before, but I suspected I was falling in love with her. I'd meant it when I'd told her that if I lost control of my bloodlust and drained her dry, I would take one of those discarded antlers and stake myself in the heart.

Annika was why I'd come to accept myself as a vampire.

She was my reason to live—and my reason to fight.

Pulling myself away from the sweet blood that flowed from her neck was easier than I ever could have imagined. The twin pinpricks from my fangs instantly healed—either as a reaction to my venom, or from her own healing abilities. Given how strong she'd been since coming into her Nephilim powers, I suspected the latter.

"That's it?" She gulped, her eyes flashing with an array of emotions.

"Usually a vampire bite feels quite pleasant," I mused, unable to help myself from smirking at the wild look in her eyes. "It's an effect of the venom. Was it not that way for you?"

"No!" She spoke quickly, touching the part of her neck where my fangs had pierced her skin. "It was." Her cheeks flushed, and I couldn't help but be amused at how off-guard I'd caught her. "I just meant—is that all you need? I thought you'd need more…"

"I usually do need more." I was quick and to the point, not wanting to embarrass her any more than necessary. "But your blood was more potent than human blood. Likely because you're Nephilim."

"It seemed like you were able to stop yourself easily," she said. "Was that also because I'm Nephilim?"

"No." My voice was husky as I gazed down upon her. "That was because you're you."

"Oh." She lowered her eyes and twisted her hands together in her lap, although she quickly looked back up to me. "Thanks."

"Don't thank me," I said. "You're the one who offered me your blood. I'm the one who's grateful to you."

The energy between the two of us was so thick that I felt it crackle in the air. I was about to lean forward to kiss her again when I saw a movement from the corner of my eye.

I leapt in front of Annika and into fighting stance, ready to face whatever was lurking in the shadows.

A stag walked out onto the beach. It held a piece of bright pink fruit in its mouth, and its big brown eyes looked at us with complete innocence.

Annika began to laugh, and her laughter was contagious—I couldn't help but chuckle as well. I felt slightly foolish for going on guard for what appeared to be a harmless stag. But after the sea creature, it was better to be safe than sorry.

Three more stags stepped up behind the first one, each with an identical piece of fruit in its mouth.

"They must have known we were hungry." Annika brightened. "The fruit smells amazing."

"You're hungry?" Guilt crushed my chest—I must have been so focused on my own thirst that I'd forgotten to think about her. It hadn't felt like long ago that we'd eaten sandwiches on the boat while watching the Northern Lights, but I really had no idea how long we'd been passed out on the beach.

"Ever since coming into my Nephilim powers, I've needed to eat more than I did when I was human," she said with a shrug. "Luckily for us, we have a welcome party."

She took a deep breath, smiling at the scent of the fruit, and skipped toward the stags. The fruit wasn't tempting at all to me—vampire tastes tended to veer toward meat, and Annika's blood had given me all the nutrients I'd needed.

But while I was happy there was food on the island, I hurried behind her and took her wrist in mine, forcing her to stop.

"What?" She glanced back at me, irritation crossing her face. "They're harmless."

"Maybe," I said. "But since we know nothing of this island, we can't be sure. What does your angel instinct tell you?"

She took a deep breath and closed her eyes, looking like she was deep in focus. "Nothing," she said, opening them again. "I can't get a read on it. Which must mean we're not doing anything dangerous, right?"

I shrugged, since I knew far less about angel instinct than she did. The Nephilim had been tricky—they'd kept the most important details about their race from all other supernaturals. Not much about them could be found in the books in the library of the Vale. When their race had gone extinct, most of the knowledge about them had died as well.

"I wish we still had our own food," I said, since I trusted the supplies that the mages had given us more than I trusted an unknown fruit brought to us by stags on a magical island.

"Well, we don't." Annika shook herself out of my grip and rushed toward the nearest stag. "And I'm hungry."

The animal dropped the fruit it was holding into her hand, and before I could say another word, she took a giant bite.

8

JACEN

Annika swallowed the fruit and blinked a few times, confusion passing over her eyes.

"We need to go back to the Haven," she said suddenly. "It isn't safe here."

Still holding onto the fruit, she raced along the beach. I was quick on her tail, but she was faster than me. Her speed didn't surprise me—the fact that Nephilim could outrun every other supernatural *was* one of the few details I'd read about them in the texts at the Vale.

But up until now, I'd never thought she would be running away from *me*.

She turned a corner around the beach, and up ahead was a small version of an old Viking boat. She leaped inside, and then she turned around, smiling when she found me standing next to the boat.

"I was hoping you'd follow." She continued to beam down at me, her eyes watery and glazed over. "Are you coming?"

I wanted to tell her that no, of course I wasn't going to leave the island—and that she shouldn't be leaving, either. But it was more than apparent what had happened. That fruit was making her want to leave the island. It reminded me of the Lotus fruit from the *Odyssey*, except it had the opposite affect. Instead of making you want to stay on the island forever—like the Lotus fruit did in the *Odyssey*—it made you want to *leave*.

I needed to get that fruit out of her system.

"Of course I am." I jumped up onto the boat to join her, and then I kissed her gently upon the lips. I made sure not to deepen the kiss, not wanting to risk ingesting any of the fruit.

She sank into my embrace, relaxing from my touch.

Before she had a chance to react, I pinned her down, bit my wrist with my fangs, and pressed the open vein to her mouth. She tried to fight me, but while Nephilim were faster than vampires, vampires were generally stronger—and I was certainly stronger than Annika.

She had no choice but to let my blood flow down her throat—my blood that was poisonous to supernaturals.

She started to cough, so I lifted my wrist and jumped off of her, not wanting to hurt her. She hurried to the side of the boat and expelled the contents of her stomach into the sea.

I turned away, wanting to give her privacy. In the meantime, I picked up the fruit she'd brought on board and chucked it overboard as well.

"Thanks," she croaked once she was finished being sick. "That fruit… it did something to me." She brought her hand to her forehead, shaking her head. "I wasn't thinking straight."

"It must have been some sort of security measure to drive people away from the island," I said. "Luckily for both of us, vampires aren't tempted by fruit."

"Then it's a good thing I asked you to join me on this mission, isn't it?"

"It is." I nodded, since if I wasn't here, I suspected she would be rowing away on the boat by now. "But for the rest of the time while we're on this island, I think we should make a pact."

"What kind of pact?" she asked.

"A pact that we won't eat or drink anything from here," I said. "Luckily, the fruit didn't physically harm you, but we have no idea what else waits for us. We need to be as careful as possible."

"Deal." She hopped out of the boat, landing softly on the sand. "But I'm hungry, so the sooner we get to the Tree, get the Grail, and get out of here, the sooner we'll be able to eat again. Let's go."

I jumped out of the boat to join her on the sand, and together, we headed toward the Tree in the center of the island.

9

ANNIKA

THE ISLAND WAS SMALL, so it didn't take long until we were nearing the Tree. Luckily, no more animals popped out of nowhere, tempting us with food that would mess with our minds.

Under the glowing green leaves of the Tree, it felt like we were in a magical forest. I couldn't help but look up in awe as we walked. A bird flew overhead—a giant eagle—but luckily, it didn't swoop down to bother us. If anything, its watchful eyes made me feel like it was looking out for us to ensure we were safely on our way. The stag horns were still everywhere—we had to be careful while walking not to trip on them—but we saw no more signs of the actual stags.

We crested a small hill, and finally saw the trunk of the Tree. It was huge—as wide as a house—with thick branches going all the way up to the top. At least I assumed they went up to the top—the top was so high up that I couldn't see it.

Jacen and I both stopped in our tracks, staring at the Tree.

Neither of us had a chance to speak before a growl echoed through the air. It was so loud that I swore the leaves on the Tree vibrated from the force of it.

I instinctively reached for my sword. "What was that?" I looked around, ready for anything.

"I don't know," Jacen said. "But it sounded like it came from the other side of the Tree."

"Then I guess we'll be heading around to investigate." I held my sword at the ready and made my way around the Tree. Jacen stayed by my side.

We rounded the corner to find a red dragon.

I stumbled back, overcome by shock. The creature was smaller than I'd imagined dragons to be—about the size of a car—and it stood on its legs, its wings flapping behind it. But it didn't try to attack. Not because it didn't want to—its feral eyes showed that it did—but because its feet were chained to the Tree, keeping it in place.

On the trunk behind it was the outline of a large door.

The creature snarled at us, showing its pointy teeth.

Luckily, fire didn't come out of its mouth, so we were safe for now.

"A dragon." I needed to voice what I was seeing out loud to make sure I wasn't going crazy—or to make sure I wasn't still under the influence of that strange fruit.

"Not a dragon," Jacen said. "A wyvern."

"A *what?*" I asked.

"A wyvern," he repeated. "They're smaller than dragons, and they have two legs. Dragons have four. Plus, dragons breathe fire. Wyverns don't. They do, however, have a taste for supernatural flesh."

"How do you know all of this?"

"I told you I did a lot of reading in the Vale." He shrugged. "The non-fiction section in the palace library was full of useful information. I had a feeling it would come in handy at some point or another."

"So to get to the door, we need to kill this wyvern before it turns us into its next meal," I said.

"Looks like it," Jacen agreed.

I tried to push away defeat at the knowledge that all the weapons the mages had supplied us with were now buried somewhere in the icy sea. With all those weapons, we would have stood a much better chance at getting past this wyvern.

"Maybe there's another way in," I said, although I couldn't help but doubt it.

"Maybe," he said. "Let's walk around the perimeter and check."

We did that, but just as I'd suspected, the door behind the wyvern was the only way in.

"At least I saved this sword." I raised the sword that I'd saved from the boat at the last minute. "We just need one good swing. Any chance you read up on the best way to kill a wyvern?"

He studied the wyvern for a few seconds. "There's a sensitive spot on the back of its neck." He placed a finger on a similar place on the back of my own neck, sending electricity through me at his touch. "Jam a weapon straight through it and into its brain, and it'll be dead."

"All right." I stepped away from him and readied my sword. "Let's get this over with."

Then I ran toward the wyvern. I couldn't let myself overthink this—I just had to trust my angel instinct and *do* it.

The wyvern hovered in the air, thrusting its wing out at me and shoving me backward.

The wing hit me like a brick wall.

I landed with my back to the ground, the wind knocked out of me. But I held tightly onto my sword, not willing to lose it as easily as I had in the fight against the sea creature.

Jacen was suddenly standing in front of me, guarding

me from another attack. I sucked in a deep breath and stood up as he reached down to grab two discarded antlers, throwing them straight into the wyvern's eyes.

The creature shrieked loudly enough to rattle the ground beneath my feet. It swatted at the antlers with its wings, pushing them out of its eyes.

Its eyes were hollowed out, gory messes. Blood dripped down its cheeks from the empty sockets. It bucked its head and shrieked again, clearly in pain.

Jacen and I backed away, clearing the area where the chains allowed the wyvern to reach.

I grabbed two more antlers and threw them toward the creature as hard and fast as I could.

They clanked against its skin, bouncing off and falling to the ground.

"A wyvern's skin is impenetrable," Jacen said. "Its only sensitive spots are its eyes and the place I mentioned on the back of its neck."

"At least it's blind now," I said. "So it won't be able to see an attack."

With that, I ran for it again, preparing to jump in the air and jam my sword through the back of its neck. Fear pulsed through me as I got closer, but I pushed it away. I was almost there. I could do this. I wouldn't be here if I couldn't.

It raised its wing, blocking me and swatting me onto the ground.

I landed hard on the pointy end of one of the antlers. I gasped in pain and looked down to find blood dripping from the gash on my leg. But I fought through the pain and jumped back onto my feet, running out of the wyvern's reach before it could go in for a second attack.

The wyvern sniffed the air and shrieked. It ran toward me until the chain around its ankle drew tight, holding it in place.

It only stopped shrieking once the wound on my leg had healed completely.

"Did you see that?" I asked Jacen, jumping in excitement at my newfound discovery.

"Did I see you recklessly try to attack the wyvern again without any thought or planning?" he asked, glaring at me. "It was pretty hard to miss."

"Not that." I brushed away his worries, since I'd ended up being fine—my Nephilim healing abilities had seen to that. "I meant the way it went crazy when I started to bleed."

"Of course it did," he said. "I told you before, wyverns have a taste for—"

"Supernatural flesh," I finished his sentence with a grin.

He looked from me to the wyvern and back again. "What're you thinking?" he asked.

"Stand over there." I pointed twenty feet away from me.

"Why?" He didn't budge from his current place by my side.

"I want to test something out," I said. "So I don't do anything *reckless* again." I couldn't resist using his previous words against him, although I gave him a small smile to let him know I was playing.

"Good," he said. "We're a team, and that means we work together. So, what's your plan?"

I was impatient to get on with it, but at the same time, I knew he was asking because he cared about me. And he was right—we were a team. That meant we needed to communicate, especially in situations like these.

"Stand far away from me—in a place where the wyvern also can't reach you—and make yourself bleed," I said. "I want to see what it does when it smells your blood."

"As do I." He smirked, realization dawning in his eyes, and he whizzed over to the spot I'd pointed to before.

His fangs pierced his skin, his blood bubbling up over the wound.

The wyvern sniffed the air and shrieked. It ran toward Jacen until the chain around its feet tightened, yanking it still and holding it in place.

Once Jacen's cut healed, the beast was placated once again.

It backed closer to the door, the tension on the chain letting up. But from the way it was sniffing the air, it was still very much aware of our presence.

If I tried to attack again, I was pretty confident I would get wing slapped to the ground for a third time.

"You're right," Jacen said, dashing back over to my side. "The smell of fresh blood sends it into a frenzy."

"But we both heal too quickly to keep our blood flowing for long," I said. "At least, not without maiming ourselves to the point where we'll be useless in a fight."

"Neither of us are going to do that." From the guarded way he was looking to me, I could tell he wouldn't accept anything other than an agreement.

"We won't," I confirmed, and he relaxed instantly. "But can you keep a wound fresh and open for a few minutes? That's all the time I'll need."

"Maybe." He watched me suspiciously. "What are you planning?"

I told him my idea as quickly as possible, since we didn't have time to waste.

He nodded once I finished explaining. "I'd tell you

that this is dangerous, but you know that already." He glanced at the monster again, his forehead crinkling in worry. "But this is what we're here for, and you have speed and stealth. If anyone can pull this off, it's you."

My heart leaped at his faith in me, and I couldn't resist pulling him in for a kiss. The fact that he was supporting me and believed in me meant more than I could ever say.

"Yes," I said, forcing myself to break away from him. We'd have more time together later. Right now, we needed to fight. "I'm ready."

ANNIKA

JACEN RAN BACK TO POSITION, and he bit his wrist again, allowing his blood to flow.

The wyvern latched onto his scent and went crazy.

Once the cut was nearly healed, Jacen bit himself again. The wyvern continued to snarl and growl, pulling at its chain like it had been years since its last meal.

Confident that the wyvern was distracted, I made my way around the Tree, being as quiet as possible. The Tree's trunk was huge, so I soon found a place that had enough divots to act as footholds.

Using them, I began to climb.

With my angel strength plus my gymnastics training, climbing the Tree was relatively easy. It didn't take long until I made it to the lowest hanging branch. The branches were thick as well, so the first one I reached had no problem supporting my weight.

I climbed and jumped my way from branch to branch until reaching one right above the wyvern's head.

Jacen was still in his spot up ahead, continuing to keep the wound on his wrist open. He glanced up at me and nodded.

I nodded back at him and took a deep breath, preparing myself for what I was about to do. I *had* to get this on the first try. I wasn't sure how smart the wyvern was, but given the way it had known I was coming when I'd rushed at it the first two times, its sense of smell was strong enough to know where Jacen and I were at all times. Jacen's blood was distracting it for now, but my best chance at success was to catch the creature unaware.

Gazing down at the wyvern from where I was crouched above it on the branch, I easily spotted the vulnerable place that Jacen had mentioned—a fleshy part below its neck. It was the only part of its body not covered in rock-hard scales.

I removed my sword from its sheath and jumped.

I landed on the wyvern's back, right below its neck. It shrieked louder and reared up, but before it had a chance to buck me off, I raised my sword and slammed it into the flesh on the back of its neck.

The wyvern crumpled beneath me, its shrieking silenced.

I somehow managed to hold on as it fell. Once it had stilled, I leapt from its back and circled around it to make sure it was dead.

From the way it wasn't moving—or breathing—it looked like it was.

Jacen zipped to my side, checking me to make sure I wasn't hurt. "Good job," he said, apparently deeming me free from any injuries.

"You did a pretty good job yourself." I smiled. "If you need any more blood…" I tilted my head and moved my hair away from my neck, hoping he got the message that he was free to take whatever he needed.

His eyes dilated as he stared down at my neck. But after a few seconds of what looked to be intense contemplation, he shook away his desire and stepped away from me.

My heart dropped—I was hoping he'd take me up on my offer. After he'd drank from me at the beach… well, I was looking forward to his doing it again.

"Soon," he promised, giving my hand a quick squeeze. Apparently my disappointment had been splattered all over my face. "But we should hurry inside. Wyverns aren't *supposed* to be able to come back to life after being killed, but there's no need to take our chances."

"All right," I said, since the *last* thing we needed was to have to fight the wyvern for a second time.

So, with my sword still in my hand, I walked to the door carved into the trunk of the Tree, reached for the handle, and pulled it open.

11

ANNIKA

WE WALKED through the door and entered an ornate, high-ceilinged ballroom.

The door slammed shut behind us, and I walked toward the center of the room, looking around in awe. The room was larger than should have been physically possible. The only sign that we were actually *inside* the Tree was that the walls and ceiling were made of intricately carved wood. The floor was pure hardwood, too.

But what stood out to me the most were the doors. The walls were lined with beautiful doors, each one of them a different color. The doors ebbed with light, as if something magical lurked behind them. There must have been at least twenty of them in all. Most of them had a handle and a lock. Only two were totally flat—a golden door and a silver door.

A glance behind me showed that the door we'd emerged from was green. Like most of the others, it had a handle and a lock.

"Did you read about this place in any of the books in the library?" I asked Jacen, continuing to gaze around the room.

"No," he said. "But none of the books mentioned the Tree of Life either. So it seems like we're in completely new territory here."

"And there's no sign of the Grail," I said.

"No," he agreed. "There isn't."

"I guess I sort of figured it would be waiting inside the Tree." I searched for a spot where the Grail might be hiding, but found nothing.

Suddenly, my angel instinct urged me to turn around.

I did just that, and came face to face with the gold door.

Of course—the door my angel instinct was apparently guiding me toward was one of the only two *without* a doorknob.

"This one." I walked toward the gold door and stared up at it. It was tall and intimidating, and I couldn't help feeling small in comparison.

"Great," Jacen said. "One of the ones without a handle."

I smiled, since I'd just been thinking the same thing.

He quickly came to my side, and the two of us stared up at the door together. He pressed his hand against it and pushed. Nothing happened. He pushed again, grunting from the force he was putting into it.

"This thing isn't budging." He dropped his hand back down to his side and shook it a few times, as if trying to get the circulation moving again.

I tried pushing the door as well, but also couldn't move it. I wasn't surprised—it was no secret that Jacen was stronger than me.

But *something* had guided me toward this door—my angel instinct—so I closed my eyes, trying to get in touch with it again.

Just like when we'd been back at the mages cabin, my instinct told me to knock.

I raised my hand and knocked three times on the intimidating golden door.

We waited a few seconds, saying nothing. All was quiet in the room. Maybe I needed to try again?

But before I had a chance, the door swung open, revealing a golden, winding staircase that led all the way to the clouds.

12

CAMELIA

I woke up in the morning with my stomach swirling. It felt like there was a lump of poison inside of it. I felt cold and hot at the same time, and my skin was coated in a fine sheen of sweat.

I jumped out of bed and ran into the bathroom, barely making it to the toilet before throwing up what felt like everything that I'd eaten last night.

Once sure that nothing else could come out, I flushed and walked to the sink, where I brushed my teeth and splashed some water on my face in an attempt to freshen up.

Witches never got sick—we were immune to human illnesses. I'd only thrown up on the rare occasions that I'd drank more alcohol than I could handle. I would normally assume this was a nasty hangover, but I hadn't been drinking recently, in case it turned out I was pregnant.

That was when it hit me. What I'd just experienced must have been morning sickness.

I hurried to where I'd stashed the potion that would make me lose the baby, and I took it out, staring at it. I already knew I didn't want to drink it, but looking at it now confirmed my decision.

I walked back to the bathroom, emptied the contents of the vial into the toilet, and flushed it away.

I could never harm the baby growing inside of me.

Except that war was coming to the Vale. The guards that Scott had sent out had confirmed it when they'd located the wolves' camp.

By staying in the Vale, I was putting my child and myself at risk.

There was only one place where we might both be safe.

The Haven.

13

CAMELIA

THERE WEREN'T many witches in the Vale, and none of them had anything close to my magical strength.

But when I called for the five strongest to come to my quarters, they arrived in minutes.

"What's this about?" the oldest one—Elizabeth —asked.

"I have urgent business to attend to outside of the Vale." I spoke quickly and confidently, not wanting them to suspect that anything was amiss. They—along with most citizens of the Vale—didn't even know that Laila was dead. There was no need to send them into a panic.

"What kind of business?" The youngest one—Jessica —spoke up. "Does it have anything to do with where Queen Laila's disappeared to for the past few days?"

That was the story the citizens in the Vale were being

told—that Queen Laila was away on a business trip. When she was alive, she went away on business often enough that no one suspected a thing.

"That's confidential." I remained as stern as possible, since questions would only lead to trouble. "But while I'm gone, I'd like for the five of you to hold up the boundary of the Vale."

As expected, doubt and confusion crossed over their eyes.

There'd only been one other time when they'd maintained the boundary—when I'd gone to Ireland to call upon the fae. Then, Laila had told the witches herself that she needed them to uphold the boundary until I returned. Laila hadn't been happy about it—I was the only witch she trusted to uphold the boundary of the Vale—but she'd wanted me to go to the fae and ask about Geneva's sapphire ring badly enough that she'd entrusted the boundary to these five witches while I'd been gone.

"Is this order from the queen?" Elizabeth was the first to speak up.

"It is." I nodded. "Since she's gone, she instructed me to tell you in her stead."

"What about Prince Scott?" she asked. "Does *he* know about this?"

"He doesn't," I snapped. "And he's not to know until

I'm gone. This is for the benefit of the Vale. Do you understand me?" I stared her down with the most intimidating look I could muster.

It was times like these that I wished I had the royal vampires' ability of compulsion. But I didn't have compulsion, so my rank as Queen Laila's second in command would have to do.

"You're to uphold the boundary around the Vale until I return," I repeated, hoping to drill the order into their minds. "Understood?"

Of course, I had no intention of *ever* returning to the Vale, but there was no way I was telling them that. Because the truth was, the five of them together couldn't create a boundary as strong as I could on my own. They knew that as well as I.

But protecting the Vale was no longer my priority.

I rested my hand flat against my stomach, knowing that from this point forward, my child would *always* come first—even before the place I'd called home for all my life.

"Understood." Jessica straightened her shoulders, appearing the most confident of the five. "When do we start?"

I glanced at the bag I'd already packed up and left next to my bed. It had all my favorite clothes, jewelry, and anything else I'd deemed valuable.

It had taken packing a bag with the knowledge that I might never return to realize how all of the *things* I owned weren't as important as I'd always believed them to be.

"You start now," I said.

I confirmed that they'd constructed the boundary, then I walked over to my bag, placed my hand on it, and teleported to the Haven.

14

ANNIKA

I GAZED up the golden stairs leading up into the clouds in more awe than I'd felt upon entering the Tree of Life.

"Together?" I asked Jacen, taking his hand in mine.

"Together," he repeated, and then we stepped through the doorway.

Well, *I* stepped through the doorway. Jacen hit some kind of invisible wall, and his hand instantly disconnected with mine.

"What happened?" I reached my arm through the door, and it passed through easily.

Jacen tried to do the same, but his hand couldn't make it through the frame. It was like there was glass blocking him from passing through. He banged his hand against it, but nothing changed.

I walked back over to his side with no problems whatsoever. "Let's try again." I reached for his hand again, focusing hard on bringing him with me as we stepped through the frame.

Like last time, I was able to walk through, but he wasn't.

"It's not letting me in," he said. "You'll have to go without me."

I frowned, looking up the stairs. "I don't want to leave you behind," I said, joining him back at the other side of the door.

He took my hands, gazing down at me with an emotion I couldn't quite place.

All I knew in that moment was that he cared about me deeply.

"This is your mission—*your* destiny," he said. "Trust me, I hate watching you go on without me. I hate knowing that if you need me, I won't be able to get to you. But out of all the doors in this place, your instinct led you to this one. There's something special waiting up there. Since I'm clearly not allowed through, it's up to you to find out what that something is."

I looked back up the golden stairway, knowing in my heart that he was right. I needed to go up there.

Jacen had been immensely helpful in getting us to

this point—I surely would have died without his help. But it was time to continue on my own.

"Stay safe," I told him, kissing him again. As we kissed, an emotion brewed in my chest—something stronger than I'd ever felt before.

Before I could figure out what it was, he pulled away and rested his forehead against mine. "You're the one who needs to be staying safe," he said. "There's no need to worry about me. I'll be waiting right here when you get back."

I smiled, since I knew he would be. There were times when I still couldn't believe that this magnificent vampire prince had given up so much for me—but this time wasn't one of them.

I walked through the doorway again, not letting go of his hands until the barrier forced them from mine.

He stepped back, and the golden door slammed shut, leaving me alone.

At first I felt afraid. Tears filled my eyes, and I pressed my hand against the door, wishing Jacen could have come with me.

But there was no point in wishing for what couldn't be. So I spun around and gazed up the winding steps, taking a deep breath to build my confidence. I wasn't getting any feelings of danger up ahead—only warmth and safety. As if a part of me belonged here—wherever "here" was.

And so, I walked onto the first step and rested my hand on the rail, beginning my trek up the golden stairs.

15

ANNIKA

THE TREK up the stairs felt like it took hours. Luckily, my Nephilim abilities stopped me from getting winded.

Eventually, I reached the bottom of the cloud. I couldn't see much after that—just a never-ending white fog—but I used the handrail to continue to guide myself up the stairs. I prepped myself for the air to feel thicker inside the cloud, but there was no difference at all.

I soon surfaced at the top of it, coming sight to sight with a man surrounded by a glowing golden aura. His skin was perfectly smooth, and in his all-white outfit, he appeared to be ageless. His eyes were gold as well. Not just a slim ring of gold around the pupils like I had as a Nephilim, but fully gold.

Just as my angel instinct let me know I was safe in

this place, it also let me know that whoever this man was, I could trust him, too.

"Annika Pearce," he said with a kind smile. "I've been expecting you."

"Hi." I wrung my hands together, unsure what else to say. A gazillion questions whizzed through my mind, but I started with what seemed like the most important ones. "Where am I? What is this place? Who are you?"

"My name is Emmanuel, and I'm an angel." His voice was smooth and melodic, like listening to a beautiful song. "Earlier, you entered the main hall of the Tree of Life, which houses the doors to the infinite realms. The one you took led you here—to Heaven."

"Heaven?" I blinked, sure I must have heard incorrectly. "As in *the* Heaven?"

"Yes, this is *the* Heaven," he confirmed.

"So I can see my family again?" My heart leapt with the possibility.

"Heaven is only for angels and for the Nephilim invited by the angels," he said. "Those who die go to the Beyond—a place veiled from the universe we know."

"So my family isn't here." My eyes watered, my burst of hope shattered.

"I'm sorry, but no," he said kindly. "Your family is in the Beyond."

"Okay," I said, since what else could I do but accept

it? I just hoped that whatever the Beyond was like, they were happy there.

"However, we're not here to talk about the Beyond," he said. "We're here to talk about you—or more importantly, about the item you seek."

"The Holy Grail." I looked around the platform where we stood, seeing only endless clouds.

"Yes." He nodded. "But as it seems you've already noticed, the Grail isn't here right now."

"Oh." I frowned. "So if the Grail isn't here, why am *I* here?"

"I might know where the Grail is," he said. "But first, aren't you interested in hearing why the Grail is needed right now?"

"I am." I brightened at the possibility that I might finally get some answers.

"I expected as much," he said. "Do you remember the moment in the Crystal Cavern when you reached for a sword to protect yourself from a swarm of bats?"

"Yes." I shuddered at the memory of those bats flying down from the ceiling and coming for me all at once.

"That sword wasn't just any sword," he said. "It was an ancient, holy object used to imprison the immortal spirit of the greater demon Samael—the last demon who walked the Earth after they were banished to Hell forever. The sword was intended to be a punishment worse than Hell. The moment you drew blood with the sword was the moment when Samael's spirit was released upon the Earth."

"What?" My hand rushed to my mouth in horror. "You mean that I released a spirit of a... demon?"

"You did," he confirmed.

Horror filled me to my bones. Had this all been an elaborate trick? Had I been led here not to retrieve the Grail, but to receive a consequence for what I'd unknowingly done?

"I never meant to do it," I said, praying he believed me. "I didn't know."

"I know that," he said, although I didn't relax yet, since that didn't mean he wasn't going to punish me. "What's done is done—there's no way to reverse what's already happened. All we can focus on now is making this right."

I finally could breathe again, since from what he was saying, I wasn't about to be smitten down by an angel, or whatever an angel would do as punishment. However, I'd still released a demon soul upon the Earth.

How could I possibly make something like that right?

"Can the demon be put back inside the sword?" I asked.

"He should be sent back to where demons belong—

to Hell," Emmanuel said. "But soon after Samael was released, he possessed the body of a young witch named Marigold. He's been using a combination of his and Marigold's powers to convince the weaker minded wolves of the Vale that they're having prophetic dreams of a Savior who will rise and bring peace and prosperity to their species. Samael has the wolves convinced that in order for this 'Savior' to rise, the vampires who live in the Vale must be eliminated."

This all sounded familiar, but at the same time, it didn't. Jacen had told me about his meeting with the First Prophet Noah, including what Noah had told him of the wolves' Savior. But from what he'd told me, both he and Noah truly believed that the Savior was legitimate.

Once I returned with the truth of what Emmanuel had told me—and a gut instinct *knew* that he was telling me the truth—it would change everything.

"If there's no Savior, then why does Samael want the vampires cleared from the Vale?" I asked.

"Because Samael wants to open a Gate to Hell," Emmanuel said. "There's a spell that can open a Hell Gate anywhere that two tectonic plates meet—such as a mountain range—but only if enough supernatural blood is spilled on that land. By encouraging the wolves to wage war on the vampires and spill their blood in the Vale, Samael can then use Marigold's body to cast the spell to open the Hell Gate. If he does that, the demons will be released onto Earth, and they'll be free to destroy your realm the same way they destroyed Hell."

He'd slammed so much information down upon me at once that I had to pause to take it all in.

"So Hell isn't a place where bad people go when they die, just like Heaven isn't a place where good people go where they die," I said, still trying to get this all straight.

"Correct," Emmanuel said. "Like I said earlier, all who die go on to the Beyond. Heaven is purely for angels, whereas Hell is purely for demons. Demons are soulless, sociopathic creatures, wired to torture and kill for enjoyment. Their realm—Hell—is locked so they can't bring their destruction to any other realms. But the demons have destroyed Hell by using up all its resources. Now it's practically unlivable, and they're desperate for a new place to live. If Samael has his way, that place will be Earth."

"We can't let that happen," I said. "Samael has to be stopped."

"The cards have already started to fall—at this point, there's no stopping what's destined to happen," Emmanuel said. "But it's *your* fate to close the Hell Gate before it's too late."

"We can't wait for the Hell Gate to be opened," I said. "We have to stop it from being opened in the first place."

"You may try," he said. "But no matter what, you're going to need to drink from this in order to have a chance at defeating Samael."

He reached down into the cloud beside him and pulled out a large, intricately designed golden chalice—the Holy Grail itself.

16

CAMELIA

I ARRIVED in the center of a lavish courtyard, where vampires, witches, and shifters dressed in matching white garments went about their daily tasks.

The moment I appeared, everyone stopped what they were doing and stared at me.

I shifted uncomfortably and tightened my grip on the handle of my suitcase. In my black leather pants and matching jacket, I couldn't have stood out more if I'd tried.

But the moment of arrival to a new place—especially a place that I intended to call my future home—wasn't the time to show weakness. So I straightened and walked to the three people nearest to me—one male vampire and two females—who were sitting on the steps hovering around a cellphone.

The man was looking at the phone as if it were a glowing meteorite that had just fallen from space.

"Hello," I said, giving them all a curt nod. "Can one of you please tell me where I can find Mary?"

I knew enough about the other kingdoms to know that despite being the leader of the Haven, Mary didn't use a formal title in front of her name. In the Haven, all were considered equal, including their leader.

"Finally, an outsider—and a witch at that." The man beamed, as if I'd landed in the Haven's courtyard straight from Heaven itself. "These two are telling me that these 'cellphones' were created by humans without the help of any magic." He gestured to the phone, like he was unsure I would know what device he was speaking about. "I think they're trying to play me for a fool. Would you mind settling this debate once and for all?"

I gave him a blank stare, unsure if this was some kind of joke or not.

"He's serious." The vampire to his left—a girl with jet-black hair who looked no older than twenty—sighed and rolled her eyes. "Just answer his question, and I'll take you to Mary."

"Cellphones were created by humans by using only science," I said simply, directing my answer more to the woman than to the man. "Now, I'd appreciate being shown to Mary."

"Sure thing." She turned to the other woman she was with—a nondescript brunette. "You'll continue acclimating Peter while I'm gone?"

"I'll do my best," she said.

"Pardon me for being such a hassle." The man—Peter —crossed his arms, looking offended. "Believe it or not, I was fascinated by science during my years. But waking up a century in the future has gotten me behind on the latest innovations..."

The dark haired vampire led me away, and I glanced back at Peter before following her toward the surrounding building.

"Did he just say that he woke up a century in the future?" I asked.

"It's a long story," she said. "I'm Elisa, by the way."

"Camelia," I replied in return.

"Camelia," she repeated, stopping in place. "As in the witch who upholds the boundary of the Vale?"

"Yes." I kept my answer short—I didn't want to explain more without Mary being present.

"I didn't think Queen Laila allowed you to leave." Elisa apparently wasn't put off by my clipped response. "If you're not at the Vale, who's maintaining the boundary there?"

"The Vale is being properly looked after," I assured

her. "I'll explain more once I have an audience with Mary."

She nodded—apparently she finally understood my hesitation to say any more right now—and led me inside a bright, ornate building. It was bustling with people, all dressed in the same white uniform.

"So, who was the man you were with when I arrived?" I returned to what I'd asked earlier, because I wanted to divert attention away from myself, *and* because I was curious. "The one who'd never seen a cellphone?"

"That was Peter," she said. "He was turned over a century ago by Princess Karina of the Carpathian Kingdom. He's been reported as dead since the Great War, but he recently awoke in Ireland, nearly starved to death and with no memories of the past century. Normally he would be King Nicolae's responsibility, but when Mary got wind of his story, she insisted on retrieving him and bringing him to the Haven."

"He was Princess Karina's mate?" I asked, since love was the most common reason why vampires turned humans.

"He was." She nodded and turned a corner, leading me down a less crowded hall.

"Interesting," I said, since technically, Princess Karina was engaged to Prince Jacen. But Princess Karina had fled the Vale soon after Queen Laila had been killed, and she hadn't been heard from since.

There was only one reason I could think of why that might be.

"Is Princess Karina here in the Haven as well?" I asked.

"I don't have the authority to answer that question." Elisa smiled and opened the door at the end of the hall. "Now, if you'll please wait here, I'll go fetch Mary…" She trailed off, staring into the room in shock.

Mary was already sipping on a cup of blood in the colorful tearoom, apparently expecting our arrival.

17

CAMELIA

"HAVE A SEAT." Mary motioned to the couch across from her. "I've been expecting you."

I glanced at Elisa, hoping to get a read on her to find out what she knew—if she knew anything at all.

The vampire merely shrugged and stepped back, closing the door to leave me alone with Mary.

I left my suitcase against the wall and sat down where Mary had instructed.

"I had some coconut water brought in for you." Mary glanced at the pitcher full of cloudy liquid in front of me. "I hear it's one of the best things one can drink while pregnant."

"What?" I backed into my seat, shocked. I hadn't told *anyone* about my pregnancy. "How did you know...?"

"I have my ways." She smirked, although it miraculously didn't come off as smug. "I also know that your intentions for coming to the Haven are pure, although I don't know what those intentions are. So please, would you care to enlighten me?"

She crossed her legs and took a long sip of blood—apparently the floor was mine.

I poured myself a glass of coconut water and took a sip, making a conscious effort not to wince at its taste. I *hated* coconut water. But I was a guest here, and the last thing I needed was to appear ungrateful, so I smiled like I enjoyed it.

"War is coming to the Vale," I told Mary, swallowing down sadness as I spoke about the possibility of the only home I'd ever known being destroyed. "The wolves outnumber us, and for reasons unknown to us they want their land back, even though they have to break the treaty they signed with us centuries ago to do so. It's not looking good for the vampires and witches that live there. I would have stayed and tried to find a solution, but..." I set my glass down and placed a hand lightly upon my stomach. "I'm not just looking out for myself anymore. You know how difficult it is for a witch of my strength to get pregnant—this might be my only chance to become a mother. I needed to do what was best for my child. Which meant coming here—to the Haven."

"You're safe here," she said. "But tell me—who's in

charge of the Vale now that Queen Laila is gone?"

"You know?" I shouldn't have been shocked—everyone who'd been in the throne room during Laila's murder knew that Annika had commanded Geneva to bring her to the Haven.

"Annika told me everything," she said.

"Of course," I said, since I'd figured as much. "Is the Nephilim still here?"

She eyed me up as she took a sip of her drink, saying nothing. "Like I said, I have valid reasons to trust that you're telling me the truth about why you're here," she said. "And I believe that a powerful witch such as yourself will be an asset to the Haven. However, if I'm to be fully up front with you about the goings on around here, we're going to have to make a blood oath."

Finally, we were getting somewhere.

"What are your terms?" I asked.

"You're to tell no one of what I'm about to tell you today unless I give you permission to do so." She studied me, her fierce gaze giving a glimpse of how she'd become a leader of one of the biggest supernatural kingdoms in the world. "Do we have a deal?"

"Yes." I nodded, my answer a no-brainer. I needed to do whatever I could to protect my child, and that meant acquiring as much information as possible from whoever was willing to offer it. "We have a deal."

18

CAMELIA

MARY TOLD me everything she knew about the wolves—about their Savior preparing to rise, and that He required all the vampires of the Vale to be gone before that would be possible. She also told me about Rosella and her prophecy.

"Annika and Jacen have left for the Tree of Life so they can acquire the Holy Grail," she concluded. "I don't know why they need it—not even Rosella knows why—but we know it's imperative to ending this war."

"It's true, then." I sat back, taking everything in. "Jacen was never on our side to begin with."

"He *is* on our side." Mary's gaze was sharp. "He's fighting for peace on the side of the Haven."

"Right." I shook my head, internally cursing my slip-up. "I'm sorry—before this moment, I lived in the Vale for my entire life. The adjustment to a new home will take some getting used to."

"I understand," she said. "But as long as you follow the rules of the Haven—which I trust you'll do, given what's at stake..." She paused to glance at my stomach. "Then I promise we'll take good care of both you *and* your child."

"Thank you," I said, more grateful than I could ever express. "I'm in your debt. If you ever need anything from me, please don't hesitate to ask."

"Trust me, I won't."

I held her gaze with mine, feeling a sense of understanding forming between us. There was also something more than understanding—there was respect.

That was more than Laila and I ever truly had with each other. There was only one thing that was important to Laila—power. She would do whatever she needed to maintain that power, even if it meant hurting those close to her.

While Laila and Mary were both leaders, the two couldn't have been more opposite from one another if they'd tried.

But even though I should have felt safe in the Haven, I still worried for the Vale. Like I'd told Mary, the Vale had been the only home I'd ever known. I didn't want anything bad to happen to it or to those within its walls.

Without me there to uphold the boundary, the Vale was more vulnerable than ever before.

There was only one thing I could think of that could protect it.

"Geneva's sapphire ring," I said. "Does Annika still have it?"

"Do you think the Nephilim would give up the ring so easily?" Mary raised an eyebrow, apparently amused by my question.

"No." I chewed on my lower lip, trying to think of another solution for the Vale. "The vampires need to leave the Vale," I said, the solution dawning on me instantly. I hadn't seen it earlier because I hadn't *wanted* to see it, but it was the only thing that made sense. "There needs to be a mass evacuation, and it must happen without delay. It's the only way they'll have a chance to live."

"I agree." Mary smiled, as if glad that I'd been the one to say it and not her. "But would their acting king support such a decision?"

"No." I knew as well as anyone that "King" Scott was just as stubborn as Laila—he'd never back down from a fight. "But I know someone who might."

"Who?" Mary watched me curiously.

"His brother," I said. "Prince Alexander."

19

ANNIKA

"The Holy Grail." I stared at the magnificent golden chalice in Emmanuel's hand, unable to believe that I was looking at the mythical object itself.

"Yes," he confirmed. "May I please borrow your sword?"

I removed my sword from its sheath and handed it over to the angel.

He used it to slice open his wrist. He didn't even wince from the pain, and he handed the sword back to me as if nothing abnormal had just occurred.

I expected blood to emerge from the wound, but instead I saw liquid gold. It was the same consistency as blood, but it had a magical glow to it, like the aura of the angel himself.

Emmanuel lifted his wrist above the Grail and let his

blood flow into the chalice. Then he handed the chalice to me.

It was heavy, although with my new strength, I was able to hold it.

"Drink," he said.

"Your blood?" I peered into the chalice, the outline of my reflection staring back at me in the golden liquid. It was the same color as Emmanuel's eyes. "Why do you want me to drink your blood?"

The first time I'd drank Jacen's blood—back when he was helping me escape the Vale—he'd let me know how it would affect me beforehand. I had no idea what would happen to me from drinking angel blood. Despite angels being holy creatures, the thought of drinking *any* type of blood without knowing what it would do to me made me squirm.

"I cannot tell you that," he said. "To have the full support of the angels, you must have faith that we have your goodwill at heart. All I can ask is that you look inside yourself and do what feels right. Your angel instinct won't help you here—this decision is meant to be yours, and yours alone."

"Okay." I nodded, still staring into the chalice, and looked back at everything that had led me up to this moment. After getting kidnapped to the Vale, all I'd wanted was to escape—and to become a vampire so I would never have to be a victim again. Then, after fate had chosen me to journey into the Crystal Cavern and retrieve Geneva's sapphire ring, I'd realized that I couldn't let all of that power go to waste. And so, I'd ventured into the palace in disguise with the lofty goal of killing Queen Laila and setting the blood slaves of the Vale free.

I'd thought that killing Queen Laila would be the ending… but little did I know that it was just the beginning. Not only were the blood slaves still not free, but the entire world was in danger from the demon that *I'd* accidentally unleashed from that sword.

Even though I hadn't unleashed Samael on purpose, I still felt like it was my job to fix it. And one big lesson I'd learned along this journey was that great things—truly great things—weren't accomplished alone. I wouldn't be here without Jacen, Mary, Rosella, and even Geneva. Trusting them and accepting their help had made me stronger.

Now, an angel wanted to help me. A literal *angel*.

I would be a fool to say no.

And so, I lifted the Grail to my lips, and I drank.

20

ANNIKA

EMMANUEL'S BLOOD traveled through my system, burning through every vein, from my head to my toes. It felt like my entire body combusted from the inside out.

It happened so quickly that I didn't even have time to scream. The next thing I knew, I was flat on my back, staring up at the never-ending sky.

Emmanuel stood before me, watching me. I had no idea where the Grail was—I must have dropped it when I fell.

"What did you do to me?" I asked, immediately assuming the worst.

What if he wasn't truly an angel, but a demon? What if I'd been being tricked this *entire* time?

But no... my angel instinct recognized Emmanuel's

spirit. It was like a magnet, but instead of pulling me toward him, it gave me a feeling of warmth and safety.

"Stand up," he commanded.

I did as he said. The pain was gone now—I felt stronger than ever.

From the intense way he was studying me, I had a feeling he was about to answer my question. So I just stood there, waiting.

"By drinking angel blood from the Holy Grail, you have become an angel," he said simply.

"What?" I blinked a few times and flexed my hands, recalling the intense burst of pain that I'd experienced before hitting the ground. "Did you *kill* me?"

"Of course not," he said. "Like I said earlier, those who die go to the Beyond—they don't come to Heaven and become angels. Angels can only be created in one of two ways. The most common way is to be born of another angel in Heaven, although this happens rarely, because the more powerful a species is, the harder it is to reproduce. The second way is what just happened to you—a Nephilim drinking angel blood from the Holy Grail in Heaven. The change is painful, but you survived it to become an angel."

"What did you mean that I 'survived' the change?" I eyed him warily. "Was there a chance that I *wouldn't* have survived?"

"There was a chance," he said. "But that's not what happened."

"I trusted you!" I screamed—I couldn't help it. "And you nearly killed me!"

"I didn't kill you," he said. "I turned you into an angel. You're immortal now."

My mouth dropped open. I was so *not* prepared for this.

"And you're not just any angel—you're an Earth angel," he continued. "There hasn't been an Earth angel for thousands of years. Not since the last one turned on Heaven and was killed for his sins. But with the Hell Gate ready to open, there was no other option except to create another. You are Earth's only hope at having a chance to fight the demons."

"What about you and the other angels in Heaven?" I clenched my fists, doing my best to rein in my instinct to panic. "Why can't you stop the demons?"

"Angels born in Heaven are not meant to leave Heaven," he said. "But you—an Earth-born Nephilim who was turned into an angel in Heaven, will be able to walk both Heaven and Earth. Thus, making you an Earth angel."

My mind swam with all of this new information. I'd barely been getting used to being a Nephilim, and now I was an angel? An *immortal*?

It was too much to take in at once.

"Are there Earth demons as well?" The question sounded ridiculous, but I had to say *something*.

"No," he said. "The demons would need the Holy Grail—or the demonic equivalent of the Holy Grail—to create an 'Earth demon,' and that doesn't exist. Although, demons *do* have an equivalent to Nephilim. They're more commonly known as shifters."

"What?" I gasped. "The shifters are *demons*?"

"They have demon blood," he said. "But unlike demons, they have a soul—which makes all the difference in the world. They're constantly battling with their demonic side—their animal side—but they're not evil like demons. In fact, like the tiger shifters have shown by protecting the Haven, they're quite capable of using their abilities for good. Never assume a shifter is an enemy just because they have demon blood. That would be a great disservice to their entire race."

"Just like one can't assume a Nephilim is good because of their angel blood," I said, remembering the death and destruction that Mary had told me the previous generation of Nephilim had brought to the supernatural community.

"Exactly," Emmanuel said. "It's important that you remember that, always."

"But in a way, the demons *could* be considered the

wolves' saviors, right?" I asked. "Since the shifters have demon blood."

"No." His eyes darkened. "Demons—*true* demons who were born in Hell—have no souls and don't care about anyone but themselves. If the Hell Gate opens, they will come to Earth and slowly destroy it. You *must* stop them. As the last Nephilim—and the first Earth angel of this upcoming era of darkness—the world will depend on you."

I took a step back—this was a lot more than I'd been prepared to handle. I'd thought my world saving would end with finding the Holy Grail.

But apparently, it was only just beginning.

"How am I supposed to stop the demons?" I asked. "I might be an Earth angel now, but a little over a year ago I was only a human. I'm not cut out for all of this."

"Yes, you are," he said. "Hand me your sword again."

I did as he said, watching as he took my sword and dipped it into the cloud at our feet. I had no idea how the cloud knew to hold us up and let other objects through—it was one of those things I figured I just needed to accept as magic.

A golden glow surrounded the sword and vanished inside of it, as if embedding the sword with some kind of angelic magic.

"You need to use this sword to kill Samael,"

Emmanuel said, handing it back to me. "The cloud is made of heavenly water, and dipping this sword in the heavenly water has infused it with magic. Only a weapon dipped in heavenly water can kill a demon. But Samael is more than just a regular demon—he's a greater demon—a type of demon that can only be killed by someone with angelic blood. As the only one with ignited angel blood able to walk the Earth, you're literally the only person alive who can defeat Samael. Do you understand?"

"Yes." I gripped the sword tightly, the weight of the responsibility heavy upon my chest. "But isn't Samael's spirit inside of Marigold's body?"

"It is." Emmanuel nodded. "Her death is necessary to stop the uprising."

I shook my head at the horror of killing an innocent person. I'd already killed the vampire guards who had brought me to see Laila in the throne room—not because they'd done anything to deserve it, but because they'd been acting under Camelia's orders to attack me. Even though I'd *had* to kill them so I could live, I still hadn't reconciled with their deaths. I didn't think I ever would.

"There has to be another way," I finally said. "Marigold didn't *ask* to be possessed by Samael. This isn't her fault."

"But she must die for the greater good." Emmanuel's golden stare was cold and final. "You need to stop Samael from opening the Hell Gate—that means killing the witch. The world is counting on you to do what needs to be done. All you need to do is look into your soul, and you'll realize what that is."

With that, he flashed out, leaving me alone at the top of the cloud.

21

CAMELIA

MUCH TO MY RELIEF, Mary was making an exception to our oath and allowing me to share what I knew with Prince Alexander. The possibility of his taking charge was the only chance the vampires in the Vale had to get out of this mess, and she didn't want them to die any more than I did.

Before bringing him to the meeting room, she provided me with the Haven's white uniform to change into and had my suitcase brought to "my cabin." I still hadn't seen my new accommodation yet—I supposed that would wait until after my meeting with the prince. But judging from the fact that *everyone* in the Haven wore the same white outfit, I had a feeling that I wouldn't be getting much more use of the clothes I'd brought with me.

I was pacing around the brightly colored tearoom when Prince Alexander arrived.

"Camelia." He stood in the doorframe when he said my name, looking at me as if I were a stranger. "What has the Haven done to you to convince you to abandon the Vale?"

"The Haven didn't do anything to me," I said calmly. "I chose to come here."

"Why?"

"Have a seat." I patted the cushion next to me. "I have a lot to tell you, and not much time."

He glared at the seat, not moving. "Scott is furious," he said. "He ordered me to bring you back to the Vale."

"I'm not coming back." I leveled my gaze with his, and he gave a short nod, as if he'd already figured that out. We both knew that if I went back there, Prince Scott—I *refused* to acknowledge him as king, even in my own mind—would take away the few privileges I had left.

I would be nothing more than a slave.

Alexander finally gave in and took a seat, as I knew he would.

"I'm with child," I said, my hand drifting to my stomach.

"What?" His eyes widened in shock. "How?"

"You've been alive for long enough to know how these things work." I chuckled.

He cracked a small smile. "You know what I mean," he said. "With vampires unable to reproduce, no male witches in the Vale, and given that you've never left the Vale until now... it means the father of your child is a blood slave."

"He is not." I crinkled my nose at the thought of reproducing with a filthy blood slave. "The father of my child is a powerful man."

"Then tell me, Camelia." Alexander leaned forward and placed his hands in his lap. "Why did you run from the Vale?"

"I didn't *run*," I said, despite the fact that I sort of did. "I came to the Haven because it was the surest way to keep myself and my child safe."

"I can understand that." His response surprised me. "But you're keeping yourself and your child safe at the expense of *everyone* living in the Vale. We need you, Camelia. Without you upholding the boundary, we're more vulnerable than ever."

"I've left five witches in charge of upholding the boundary," I said, although my voice wavered, since their powers combined weren't even half as strong as mine.

"I know the five," he replied. "They're inexperienced,

and the wolves have a powerful witch at their disposal. The moment the wolves realize you're gone…"

"They'll attack," I said. "I'm well aware. They won't retreat until all the vampires are dead. It's the only way for their Savior to rise."

"What?" Alexander flinched—I'd caught him by surprise, just like I'd intended. "What do you know that you're not telling me?"

"I've learned a lot in the short time I've been in the Haven," I said.

From there, I told him all I knew about the wolves, their visions, and their Savior—the Savior that had promised to give everything to the wolves once the wolves destroyed the vampires.

22

CAMELIA

"So there's no hope in convincing the wolves to stand down," Alexander said once I'd told him everything. "They're determined to slaughter us."

"They're determined to get the vampires off their land," I corrected him. "That can happen without bloodshed."

He was silent for a few seconds—I hoped he was seriously considering his options.

"You heard Scott and Stephenie," he finally said. "They won't retreat. The land is rightfully ours in accordance to the treaty with the wolves. If we leave and allow the wolves to have it, we'll lose the respect of all the other kingdoms."

"If you leave, you'll be alive." My voice was sharp—I was determined to drive this point home. "Scott's pride won't let him realize that he'll lose the war, but you're smarter than that. We both know the facts. Our numbers are tiny in comparison to the wolves, and the majority of our citizens are untrained fighters. Yes, they're naturally strong as vampires, but that means nothing without proper training. If Jacen had made an alliance with one of the other kingdoms, we might have had a shot, but he blew it by falling for the Nephilim girl from a false kingdom."

"And there's no way of tracking them?" Alexander asked. "Are you sure?"

"I'm sure." I huffed. "They're either protected by a powerful cloaking spell or are in a location with a barrier against tracking. Maybe both. Either way, they're impossible to find."

"So Geneva's ring is lost to us." For the first time since he'd arrived, fear flashed in Alexander's eyes.

"Until they reveal themselves, that's correct. We can't track the ring if we can't track them."

"There has to be some way..." He trailed off, glancing around the room as if searching for an answer in its walls.

"There is," I said. "You can step up and be truthful with the citizens of the Vale about everything you know, and that includes letting them know about Queen Laila's death. Evacuate before it's too late. The wolves don't want the vampires dead—they just want you off the land that they consider theirs."

"The land that they signed away to us," he said.

"With their Savior ready to rise, they don't see it that way anymore," I said. "And there's so much empty land down south in America that *isn't* already claimed by shifters. Lead the people there and find a place to settle down. Be the ruler that they need. Sure, it won't be as luxurious as the Vale at first, but at least you'll be alive to turn it into something magnificent."

He was silent for a few seconds—Prince Alexander always thought before he spoke. "It's tempting when you say it like that," he said. "Except that they won't follow me. They won't leave their homes behind."

"You can't know that unless you try."

"And what about what you said before?" he asked. "About how the kingdom needs an original vampire to lead them—not a prince?"

"What the people need is a leader who will protect them—not one who will leave them ignorant in a land where they'll surely die," I said. "Prove to them that you're that leader. Do that, and you'll have their loyalty."

"What about the other kingdoms?" he asked. "They're all led by original vampires. *If* I do this—and that's a big if—will they accept my new kingdom as legitimate?"

"I can't say," I said. "It'll likely be an issue you'll have to address in the future. But at least if you get that far, you'll *have* a future."

He laid his hands in his lap and looked off to the side, appearing deep in concentration. I could practically see the wheels whirring in his brain.

"Scott and Stephenie aren't going to like this," he finally said, his eyes meeting mine once more.

"Scott and Stephenie are your *equals*," I said. "You can't cater to them and stay silent any more. Too much is at stake here."

"Okay." He nodded. "I can try. But if I do—and if I succeed—will you consider joining us as the witch of the new kingdom?"

I sat back in surprise, wanting to say *absolutely not*.

At the Haven, there was a chance that my baby could be protected from being taken by Prince Devyn once he or she came of age. But I wasn't comfortable sharing that information with Alexander yet.

So I decided to stick with my other reason—it was solid enough as it was.

"I'm sorry, but I cannot," I started, making sure to stay steady as I spoke. "As you know, maintaining a boundary as strong as the one around the Vale is meant to be a task required of multiple witches. I'm strong enough to do it on my own, but it cost me years of my life. I don't know how much longer I have left. I'll likely die young, like my mother and all my ancestors before her. Which is why I still plan on being turned into a vampire—*after* the baby is born, of course. I hope you can understand."

"I understand." He nodded. "But I had to at least ask."

"The witches who are currently maintaining the boundary have high aptitude," I told him. "With enough practice, they'll be able to uphold a boundary as strong as the one I was able to hold on my own. Also, they're not warriors by any means, so they're terrified of the possibility of an attack. Convince them to come with you. I know them well enough to believe they will."

"But if they come with me, there won't be any witches protecting the Vale," he said. "Our home will be open to an attack."

"Which is why it's imperative that everyone listen to you and evacuate."

"All right." He sat straighter—I could tell he'd made up his mind. "This new information has made what I need to do clear. Call in the witch who brought me here and tell her that I'm ready to return to the Vale."

23

KARINA

AFTER THE TRAVEL DAY—*DAYS*—I just had, I was really missing the convenience of being teleported by a witch. Bad weather had resulted in plane delays and cancellations like I couldn't believe, and it had taken over twenty-four hours for me to get from Ireland to western Canada.

It was night when I arrived at the wolves' camp—late enough that minus the guards on shift, they were all asleep. The guard on duty recognized me and instantly let me inside.

Once there, I hurried to Noah's tent.

He jumped out of bed when I let myself inside, on guard and ready for a fight. His hair was messed up from sleeping, and his shirt was off, displaying his rock solid abs. He was so frustratingly gorgeous that I wanted to jump into his arms then and there.

"Relax," I said with a smile. "It's me."

"Karina." He breathed out my name in relief. "I didn't think I would ever see you again…"

I couldn't resist for a moment longer—I closed the space between us and pressed my lips to his.

He leaned into me, his taste spicy and woodsy, and I smiled at how he'd apparently wanted me as much as I wanted him.

"Wait." He pulled away, his eyes a mix of emotions. "What happened with Peter?"

"With who?" I reached for his hands, not wanting to break contact with him after having just showing him how I felt.

"Peter," he repeated. "The man who you love. Your soul mate."

"I don't know what you're talking about." I frowned, insulted that he was ruining this moment by being so confusing. "*You're* the one I want to be with. I trust you with my life. I know it's crazy—I would have thought it was crazy if someone had told me weeks ago that I was going to care so much for a wolf—but it's true."

My cheeks heated, and I turned my eyes down, embarrassed for confessing so much. The Carpathian Kingdom taught us to *always* hide our emotions—to treat them like weaknesses. But I didn't want to do it anymore. And with war coming… well, I didn't want to think about the worst, but how could I not?

I needed Noah to know how I felt about him before it was too late.

"I think I'm falling for you." I lifted my eyes to meet his confused gaze, my hands still clasped in his. "Actually, it's more than that. I *have* fallen for you."

"No." He yanked his hands out of mine and stepped back, glaring at me.

My heart slammed to the floor at his rejection.

"Something must have happened to you at the Haven." He shook his head, his dark hair falling over his forehead. "Do you truly not remember Peter?"

"I have no idea who Peter is." Tears prickled my eyes —frustration. And hurt at how after putting all my emotions out there for Noah to see, he was barely even acknowledging what I'd said to him. "You keep saying his name, but I've never met him!"

"All right." He took a deep breath, his eyes shining with what I swore was reluctance. "I think we both need to sit down."

I went over to sit on his bed, and he took the chair across from me. My heart fell again—I'd hoped he would sit next to me.

There was only one explanation for the way he was distancing himself—he didn't return my feelings.

I was an idiot for being so open about how I felt. This was why I usually kept my feelings to myself. If I kept them to myself, then I couldn't get hurt.

"You told me everything about Peter," Noah started, his voice slightly shaky as he spoke. "You met him on a trip you took—a ship that went from Europe to America."

"I did go on a transatlantic voyage a long time ago," I said. "On the *Olympic*. However, I don't recall meeting anyone by the name of Peter."

"You met him on the deck while the ship was setting sail." Noah was speaking frantically now, as if begging me to remember this man who didn't exist. "You spent the entire trip with him. At the end of the journey, he proposed. But he didn't know you were a vampire, so you told him and gave him two options. He could either turn into one as well, or to allow you to compel away his knowledge of the supernatural—and of you. He chose to become a vampire. You turned him, and the two of you got married. You were in love and happy... until he was killed by wolves during the Great War. That's why you've been determined to get your hands on Geneva's sapphire ring—you wanted to wish for Peter to come back."

Noah sounded so convinced that I believed he thought all of this was true. He had no reason to make up such a detailed story.

But when the *Olympic* had set sail from Europe, I'd stood on the deck by myself. I'd spent a lot of time by myself on that trip, or with the vampire chaperone who had accompanied me, since it was unheard of for a lady to travel alone in that era. And above all else, I was most certain that no one had proposed to me on board. *Surely* I would remember such a thing.

No one had proposed to me, ever.

Over a century of living, and I had yet to experience love.

Maybe my feelings for Noah weren't love after all.

Maybe I was just longing for something I'd never had.

"Are you remembering?" Noah watched me with so much hope in his eyes, as if everything in the world depended on me remembering this Peter.

"It's a lovely story," I told him sadly. "But it's not real, even though you seem convinced that it is. Perhaps..." I twisted my fingers around themselves, feeling bad for what I was about to say.

"Perhaps what?" he asked.

"Could this be one of your visions from the Savior?" I asked. "Could you be mistaking a vision for reality?"

"These aren't visions." His voice was hard and confident. "You told me all of this yourself. The memories must be there somewhere. You have to at least *try* to remember them."

He watched me with so much hope that I couldn't say no.

And so, despite knowing it would be hopeless, I tried.

24

KARINA

I TRIED and was met with nothing.

"The story you told me never happened." I moved to get up, feeling more frustrated than ever. "It's just that— a story. And I didn't come to you to be bombarded by a make believe past. I came to you because I don't know why I went to the Haven, or why I called for the fae. I was hoping you would be able to help me fill in the gaps, but all you want to do is talk about this 'Peter' who doesn't even exist."

"The fae?" He tilted his head, clearly caught off guard by my mention of them. "Why did you call for the fae?"

"I don't know!" I knitted my hands in my hair, since I'd already *told* him that I didn't know. "The fae girl was already waiting for me—she knew I was going to come.

We talked, but I don't remember what we talked about. One moment she was there, then she was gone, and I was standing there alone, clueless about why I'd gone there in the first place."

Realization—mixed with possibly pity—crossed his gaze, and he walked over to sit with me on the bed. He left space between us, making sure not to touch me.

I drew inward, hating that he was treating me like a leper.

"The fae are known for driving hard bargains," he said slowly, his gaze locked on mine. "They're also apparently fond of collecting memories."

"What are you saying?" I asked. "Do you think the fae girl took my memories?"

It would certainly explain why I was so confused about why I'd sought out the fae at all.

"All I know of the fae are the legends told by my people," he said. "The shifters refuse to interact with them. We know that if you make a deal with the fae, you always give more than you bargained for."

"Okay." I sat back, thinking. "Since the shifters refuse to interact with the fae, could I have gone to them on your behalf?" I asked. "Is there something you needed that you could only get from them? Something I would have gone to them for without telling you?"

"No," he said. "Now that the packs have come

together, we far outnumber the vampires. We're going to win this war. All we need is a way to get past the boundary."

"Maybe that's what I bargained for," I said. "A way to get past the boundary."

"You didn't," he said simply. "You were determined to get Peter back, no matter what. *That's* what you went to the fae for."

"To raise him from the dead?" I raised an eyebrow. "That's insane."

"Insane or not, that was your goal," Noah said.

"But no one's ever returned from the Beyond." I shook my head in disbelief. "It's not possible."

"That's what I thought, too," he said. "But you were so determined that I couldn't crush your hope. It wasn't my place to stop you—even though all I wanted was for you to stay here, with me."

"You did?" I swallowed, not having expected him to say that.

"Of course I did." He shook his head and smiled slightly, like he couldn't believe I'd ever thought otherwise, and moved closer to me. "I fell for you the first moment I saw you, when you sneaked out of the palace to meet me at the boundary line. But your heart's never been mine. It's always belonged to Peter."

"I don't even *remember* Peter," I said. "My heart can't

belong to someone I don't remember."

"I get that." Wildness crossed over his eyes—pure, heated desire—and electricity crackled between us. "And trust me, you have no idea how hard it is for me to not be glad you don't remember him so I can finally have you as mine."

"So what's stopping you?" I tilted my head, teasing him.

"It feels wrong." He sighed and leaned his head back, as if struggling with his own urges. "Like I would be taking advantage of you. I'd never be able to forget that once you learned Peter couldn't return from the Beyond, you had your memories of him erased because you couldn't live knowing that you'd never see him again—"

"Hold up." Now *I* was the one holding a hand up to stop *him* from continuing. "I might not remember Peter, but I know myself. I would *never* give up my memories of anyone—especially someone I loved—because I couldn't deal with the grief of their loss. I wouldn't throw away something so important like it never mattered at all."

"But you did," he insisted. "Or you wouldn't have forgotten him."

I held his gaze, feeling like we were at a standstill. "Perhaps I *did* bargain away my memories of this Peter,"

I said, since it was the only explanation that made sense. "But I can assure you it wasn't because I didn't want to deal with my grief. There was another reason. There had to have been…"

I paused to think, when suddenly, a plane sounded overhead. It was so loud that it was clearly taking off or landing at the Vale.

It wasn't abnormal—the Vale used planes to receive supplies—but it was annoying in the middle of our intense conversation.

Worry crossed over Noah's eyes, and his brow creased, as if something wasn't adding up.

"What's wrong?" My hand rushed to cover his, and I was relieved when he didn't move away.

"The Vale has a strict supply schedule," he said. "We track when the planes come in and out to prepare for our attack. They shouldn't be sending out another for at least two days."

"What do you think it means?" I could only assume the worst—that they were gathering something for the upcoming war. Supernaturals rarely used human technology while fighting—we preferred to relay on our natural abilities and strength—but the vampires of the Vale were desperate.

Who knew how far they would go to win?

"I have no idea," he said. "But it can't be anything good."

Suddenly, someone unzipped the tent and stepped inside. Marigold. Her hair fell in long, unbrushed waves down her back, and she wore a white nightgown that hung to her feet. It made her look like an angel.

Noah pulled his hand out of mine and put space between us again, as if we'd been caught doing something wrong. "Yes?" he asked the witch.

"The Vale's protections are down." Marigold's eyes gleamed with excitement. If she noticed that she'd interrupted a moment between Noah and me, she didn't show it.

"What do you mean?" I asked. "How could they go down? What did you all do?"

"I don't know," she said. "I wish I could say that we'd gotten to their witch and killed her, but we didn't. All I know is that the boundary went down after that plane took off. Now, the Vale is completely unprotected."

As she spoke, something twisted in my stomach. Guilt.

Could this have happened because of me? Because of the bargain I'd made with the fae?

"What's the plan?" Noah stood at alert—a soldier ready for battle.

"We're going to wait until daylight, since that's when the vampires are at their weakest," she said. "It gives us a few hours to prepare. Then, once the sun rises, we'll soak the soil with the blood of the vampires so our Savior can finally rise."

25

ANNIKA

I MADE my way back down the golden steps, relieved that the door to the Tree of Life opened when I placed my palm upon it.

Jacen waited in the center of the room. I'd only been gone for a few hours, but from the way he beamed at me, one might have thought it had been weeks.

"Annika." He hurried toward me, but halfway there, he stopped in his tracks. "Your eyes," he said, looking at me in wonder. "They're completely gold now."

"I drank from the Holy Grail." The words didn't feel real as they left my mouth. "I'm an angel now. Well, technically an 'Earth angel.' But still an angel."

"What?" His brows shot up, panic registering on his face. "How's that possible?"

I filled him in on everything Emmanuel had told me

in Heaven. It was a lot to cover, but I did it as quickly as I could, since right now, the Vale needed our help.

"We need to get to the Vale at once," Jacen said once I was done. "I need to talk to Noah. Once he knows the truth, he'll *have* to get the wolves to stand down."

"If he believes you," I said.

"I'll make a blood oath promising him that I'm telling the truth." Jacen's eyes swam with intensity. "I know you haven't met Noah yet, but even though the shifters are technically part demon, he's a good guy. He'll believe me."

"I trust your judgment," I said, especially since Emmanuel had told me not to discredit the shifters because of their demon blood. "But how are we going to make it to the Vale in time? All we have now is that lousy rowboat I found on the beach. It'll take forever to reach the mainland in that. Unless…" I trailed off, not sure it would be possible.

"Unless what?" Jacen asked.

"Once we were done talking, Emmanuel flashed out," I said. "He teleported, like witches can do."

"And you're an angel now." Jacen brightened—he must have realized where I was going with this. "Do you think you can teleport too?"

"I have no idea." I shrugged, since I knew little about the abilities I had as an angel. "But I can try. Do you know anything about what the witches do when they teleport?"

"They need to picture where they want to go," he said. "It's more accurate if they've been there before, or if they've seen a picture."

"Then it's a good thing I've been to the Vale." I took a deep breath, holding Jacen's hand in mine.

Then I realized—by going to the Vale, we'd be near humans. Jacen had spilled a lot of his blood to distract the wyvern, and it had been hours since he'd fed.

"What's wrong?" he asked, tilting his head in concern.

"You should feed." I brushed my hair to the side, bearing my neck to him. "To be at your full strength."

"Annika..." He sounded like he was trying to resist, but his fangs emerged from his gums, showing me that I was right—he needed more blood.

I stood on my tiptoes to get closer to him, my stomach flipping in anticipation of his bite.

"You're not a Nephilim anymore." From the way his eyes were swirling with desire, I could tell it was taking everything he had not to bite me immediately. "You're a full angel. We have no idea what your blood will do to me."

"My Nephilim blood gave you more strength than

human blood," I said. "I imagine that angel blood will be even better."

"Just a sip…" He pressed his lips to my neck, and a shudder rolled through my body as he sank his fangs into my skin.

Ecstasy poured through me, and I felt more connected to him than ever. But it was over too soon. He'd barely taken anything compared to last time before pulling away.

"That's all?" I nuzzled into him, already feeling the bite marks on my neck healing.

"You were right." His breathing was heavier, his pupils dilated as he stared down at me. "Angel blood was even more delicious than Nephilim blood." He swooped down to kiss me, his tongue brushing mine. I tasted what I assumed was my blood. It was sweet, like honey.

But as much as I wanted to kiss him forever, I soon forced myself to pull away.

"In the future, you can have it whenever you want." I smiled, feeling a certain power at knowing how tempting he found my blood. "But if we don't get to the Vale, we might not *have* a future to look forward to. So… are you ready to get out of here?"

"You know it." He reached down for my hands, watching me with confidence. "Let's do this."

26

ANNIKA

I SQUEEZED my eyes shut and thought of the Vale.

It didn't feel like anything happened. But after giving it a few more seconds, I peeked to see if we'd teleported without realizing it.

We still stood in the center hall of the Tree of Life. Disappointment filled my chest. I'd been so confident a minute ago that I could get us to the Vale. Now, the Vale seemed as far away as ever.

"It didn't work," I told Jacen. "I pictured the Vale, but we're still in the Tree."

"Did you think about *wanting* to go there when you were picturing it?" he asked.

"No," I said. "I just pictured the Vale."

"Try again," he said. "This time, think about how

much you want to bring us there. Imagine us arriving into the picture in your mind."

This time, when I pictured the Vale in my mind, I also thought about how badly I wanted Jacen and I to be there and imagined us appearing.

Suddenly, my stomach swooped—like on the drop of a roller coaster. It was the same thing I'd felt when Camelia had transported me to the Crystal Cavern. We didn't really "land" as much as that I felt a subtle change in the texture of the floor beneath my feet, and the air became colder and drier.

I opened my eyes and smiled at my familiar surroundings.

We'd arrived in the attic of the Tavern. There was a blanket bunched up beneath the window, and all the books on the shelf were untouched, including the book-marked one I'd left on top of it the night I'd first brought Jacen here.

"I did it!" I squealed. "Open your eyes."

"Hell yeah you did it." He swung me around in a cele-bratory circle and pulled me in for a kiss.

Despite wanting to fall down with him onto the blanket and forget about the rest of the world, I forced myself to pull away. After all, we had a lot to do, and no idea how much time we had to do it.

"Why'd you choose to bring us to the Tavern?" he asked.

"I didn't," I said. "I was picturing the Vale in general, and ended up here."

He reached into his pockets, and it was impossible to miss the worry that crossed over his eyes.

"What's wrong?" I asked.

"My phone's still back at the Haven," he said. "I have no way of contacting Noah."

My heart plummeted—why hadn't we thought of that? We'd been so determined to get to the Vale that we hadn't thought through our plan.

"Maybe my angel instinct can help," I said. "It should be stronger now that I'm a full angel."

"It got us this far," he said. "Give it a try."

Noah, Noah, Noah, I thought, trying to hone in on the wolf I hadn't met. *How can we get to you?*

I instinctively reached for the handle on the floor— the one that pulled open the hatch that led to the rooms above the Tavern.

"This is the way out," I told Jacen. "Come on."

"Can't we just leave through the window?" he asked.

I was instantly reminded of the first night we'd met —when we'd sneaked our way inside through the very same window. It was crazy how long ago that felt—like an entire lifetime ago.

"We could," I said. "But I feel like we should go this way."

He glanced warily at the open door. "If the humans see us, they might report us to the vampires," he said. "We can't risk being stopped by Scott or Stephenie."

"The humans here are my friends," I said. "And anyway, look at us." I motioned to our clothes, which were torn and bloodied from the creatures we'd fought on our journey to the Tree. "We have no chance of blending in. The humans here don't have much, but I'm sure there's something they can loan us."

We made our way down the ladder and into the girls' dorm—the place I'd slept when I'd lived here. I didn't bother to be too quiet. Since it was night, no one would be in the dorms. The Vale kept a nocturnal schedule, so night was when most humans were working. They wouldn't come up here to start getting ready for bed until sunrise.

I nearly jumped out of my skin when I saw three girls huddled in the corner.

They stared right back at me, looking like they'd seen a ghost. I knew them from my time working in the Tavern—Jill, Rachel, and Laura—although I hadn't been close to any of them. They'd been born in the Vale and had lived there for their entire lives. They knew nothing of freedom.

When Jacen jumped down behind me, sheer terror crossed their faces.

"Your Highness," Jill sputtered, glancing back and forth between the two of us. "And Annika. You're not dead?" She stepped in front of the other girls, as if trying to protect them.

"No." I couldn't help but laugh, but I forced myself to be serious. I couldn't blame them for being confused. "Too much has happened to explain, but we're here to help you. What're the three of you doing up here now? Don't you need to be working?"

"Everything's been crazy since we found out that Queen Laila died," she said.

"What?" My eyes bulged—I hadn't expected them to know that Laila was dead. From what Jacen had told me, Scott and Stephenie were determined to keep Laila's death quiet for as long as they could.

"Who's leading the Vale now?" Jacen asked.

"Prince Scott," Jill said. "Well, I guess he's *King* Scott now. But that's not the craziest part. A few hours ago, Prince Alexander gathered everyone in the village and told us the most unbelievable story."

From there, she detailed everything that Prince Alexander had told them—the entire truth, or at least what he knew of it. Which meant everything except the reality of who the "Savior" truly was.

I listened closely, proud of Alexander for going against his siblings and telling the citizens of the Vale the truth. I didn't know much about the prince, but he sounded like he would be a *much* better leader than Scott or Stephenie.

"Prince Alexander gave us a choice," Jill finished. "Follow him to start a new kingdom in America, or stay here and face the wolves."

"Why didn't you *leave*?" I asked, unable to fathom why anyone would stay.

"Who's to say the prince is telling the truth?" Laura spoke up, her voice soft.

"Exactly." Jill nodded at Laura, backing up her friend. "Plus, everything we have is here. We can't just leave with no idea where we're going. Who's to say we'll be better off there than here?"

"You would be," Jacen said. "Alexander was correct when he said that the wolves far outnumber the vampires."

"But the vampires keep us safe," the youngest girl, Rachel, said. "They're the most powerful creatures in the world. They'll protect us, like they always do."

"They've never kept you safe," I shot back. "They kept you here unwillingly, as slaves."

"They keep us housed, clothed, and fed." Jill placed

her hands protectively on Rachel's shoulders. "We need to be thankful for what we have."

"They've taken away your freedom!" I dropped my arms to my sides, unable to stay calm for a moment longer. "You're nothing more than cattle to them. All they care about is your blood. How have you not realized that yet?"

"The human world isn't any better." She crossed her arms, jutting her chin out stubbornly. "It's worse. In the human world, they don't care if you live or die. Terrible things happen to people on a regular basis there. Society will leave you hungry and homeless. Here, I'll always have food, and I'll always have a roof over my head. I won't get overlooked like I would if I lived out there."

I pressed my lips together in frustration. This was the type of propaganda the vampires of the Vale fed to the humans who lived here on a regular basis. The ones who had been born and raised here—like Jill, Laura, and Rachel—tended to easily buy into it.

"What about Martha?" I glanced to the bed where the girl had always slept—she was the youngest and smallest at the Tavern. I used to sneak her candy bars on the days we were forced to donate blood. "Did she go with Alexander?"

"She did." Jill frowned. "Alexander promised the

humans who went with him that they would be treated as equals to the vampires—that they would even eat the same food. *That* was what convinced Martha. We all know how much she loved food. Most of the Vale-born stayed."

"You should have gone," I repeated, even though I had a feeling that getting through to them would be impossible. They were far too brainwashed for me to change their minds now.

"There's nothing for us out there," Jill said. "Alexander doesn't even know exactly where he's leading the people who followed him. They'll probably all end up dead."

"You're wrong." Jacen stepped forward and snarled. "Staying was the stupidest thing you could have done. You have *no* idea what's coming. The ones who will end up dead are the ones who stayed here. The ones like *you*."

Terror washed over the girls' faces, and I placed a hand on Jacen's arm in the hint that he needed to back down.

He sucked in a deep breath, but then he moved closer to me, managing to get control over his temper.

"We know what's coming." Jill spoke calmly and surely. "The wolves want our land, and they're going to try to fight for it. But the vampires can beat them. The vampires have held this land for centuries. That isn't going to change now."

"This is different," I said, and then as quickly as possible, I told them about Samael and his plan to use the wolves to open the Hell Gate.

As I spoke, their faces grew paler and paler.

"We're going to try to stop Samael before he can open the Hell Gate," I said once I'd told them everything. "But it's not a given that we'll succeed. And if the demons get out, you need to be as far away from here as possible."

"But there's no way out anymore." Jill shook her head and took Laura and Rachel's hands in hers. She finally looked as scared as she should have felt this entire time. "The last plane has already left."

27

STEPHENIE

I PACED AROUND my quarters as I sipped a fine red vintage mixed with blood, unable to get rid of the sense of despair crawling over my skin.

I couldn't stop thinking about everything Alexander had told the citizens of the Vale. At the time, I'd stood proudly with Scott to the side, unwilling to give up my home so easily.

Vampires had ruled the Vale for centuries. This land was *ours*. The wolves had willingly given it to us in the treaty.

Why should we run away the moment they tried to rebel and take it back? If we did that, we would always be seen as cowards. As *weaklings*.

But Alexander's words continued to tear through my

mind without relent. War was coming. The wolves outnumbered us—not only that, but they were fighting for a cause they believed in with their hearts and souls.

They were going to destroy us.

And here I was, waiting for death because I couldn't give up my pride.

I'd never been a particularly emotional person. But as I looked around my elegant quarters and out the window as the sun peaked above the snow-capped mountains, it hit me that this beautiful place that I'd called home since being turned into a vampire decades ago was about to be destroyed.

Everything I owned would be torn to shreds.

Not like it would matter, since I would most likely be dead.

But I wasn't dead yet. And I didn't *want* to die.

And so, I placed my glass down, left my quarters, and hurried down the hall toward the wing of the palace where the witches lived. Guards watched me pass, but no one stopped me.

There were only six rooms in the witches' wing. Camelia had the largest quarters—the only ones with a double door entrance.

I sneered at those doors, furious at the witch for abandoning us when we needed her most.

The other five doors were plain and simple—they were where the other five witches lived. The ones who were currently upholding the boundary around the Vale. The sun was rising, which meant they should be in their rooms getting ready for bed.

I didn't know which of them lived in which room. I just stepped up to the closest door and knocked.

There was no answer.

I knocked again, figuring she might not have heard me. Still, nothing. So I moved on to the next door. Same thing.

I knocked on all five doors, but got no answer at any of them.

This was ridiculous. Normally, I would ask a guard in the palace to find out where the witches had gone, but I didn't want anyone to know that I was looking for a witch. They might start asking questions, and questions were the last thing I needed.

So I removed a pin from my hair, stuck it inside the lock, and started to fiddle. I'd initially learned how to pick locks because it was the best way to spy on any of the guys I was dating who might be cheating—but the skill had proven itself handy in other situations too.

The locked clicked into place and I swung the door open.

As suspected, no one was inside. But hangers and clothes were strewn everywhere, as if whoever lived here had haphazardly packed for a trip at the last minute. One peek in the bathroom showed that all the essentials—toothbrush, toothpaste, shampoos, and such —were gone too. And the room still smelled like perfume. Whoever had left had left recently.

The departure was perfectly timed with Alexander encouraging citizens to follow him out of the Vale.

I picked up the closest hanger and threw it across the room with so much force that it dented the wall. But then I took a few deep breaths and looked in the mirror, trying to relax. After all, I was trying to leave the Vale, too. I couldn't blame the witch for doing the same thing that I was doing myself.

Luckily, there were still four more witches left. But I went from room to room, finding the same thing in each one—a whirlwind mess that signified a quick departure.

They were gone. *All* of them.

My conniving brother must have convinced them to go with him. He must have sneaked them onto that last flight without warning Scott or me.

There wasn't a witch left to transport me to the Haven.

More importantly, there were no more witches here to uphold the boundary. The Vale was exposed. There was no way out. I was trapped, surrounded by blood-thirsty wolves who were going to destroy my home and kill us all.

There was nowhere for me to go.

I dropped down to the floor and screamed.

28

KARINA

THE SUN ROSE in glorious pinks and yellows above the palace of the Vale.

I marched behind rows upon rows of wolves, with a bag full of necessary materials on my back and my sword strapped to my side. Noah walked on one side of me and Marigold on the other.

The wolves were still in their human forms—they were careful to shift only when necessary, to help them hold onto their humanity. The longer they remained in wolf form, the more their animalistic tendencies took over.

I should have been excited—this was the moment we'd been waiting for. However, each step I took toward the Vale filled me with dread.

I wanted to call out to the wolves to stop. But who was I to do that? I was a stranger among their kind—I owed them everything for accepting me into the pack so easily. And even if I did try to stop this, they wouldn't listen to me.

"Are you okay?" Noah asked from beside me. His eyes were kind and full of worry—my feelings must have been splattered all over my face.

"I'm fine." I forced a small smile. "Just worried, that's all."

"Rumors say you're an incredibly lethal fighter," he said. "You honor my people by siding with the pack. And… your support means a lot to me, too."

Despite the fact that we were marching into war, my heart gave a small flutter at his statement.

I got ahold of myself a second later. Now wasn't the time to be acting like a young schoolgirl with a crush.

Now was the time to focus on keeping myself—and Noah—alive.

"Stop!" Marigold called out to the crowd.

On cue, the wolves stopped marching, turned around, and faced her. She was so short that I doubted most of them could see her, but they waited for her command anyway. As they looked toward her—toward *us*—there was one common thing I noticed in their eyes.

Hope.

"Remember—go for the vampires first!" Marigold called out to the pack. "Ignore the humans. The humans are insignificant, since it's the vampires the Savior needs wiped from this land. From *your* land."

Nods of approval scattered throughout the crowd, and the wolves shifted in place, clearly ready for battle.

"Are you ready to get your land back?" Marigold was screaming now, her hand raised to the air as she commanded her army. "Are you ready for your Savior to rise?"

A chorus of "yes" and "we're ready" sounded from the crowd, many of them raising their fists to match Marigold's stance.

"That's what I thought." She smiled in approval. "Now, it's time to shift into your true selves. It's time to take back what's rightfully yours."

The soldiers shifted into their wolf forms. One of them howled, followed by another and another, until their angry howls echoed across the mountain.

Noah shifted as well, letting out a howl of his own.

It wasn't long until Marigold and I were the only ones left in human form.

"Go!" Marigold called, her eyes gleaming in excitement.

I shivered at the sight of how much glee she was getting from this.

"Have no mercy!" she continued. "And remember to leave no vampires alive!"

The wolves howled again, and then they ran toward the town to attack.

29

MARIGOLD

I'D BEEN FIGHTING the demon for so long now.

No matter what I did—no matter how hard I tried to gain control—his hold on me was too strong.

Fighting him was exhausting.

I watched as he used my body to lead the wolves toward the palace to murder the vampires, and it was too much. I couldn't continue on like this, as a puppet in my own body, observing the atrocities I was being forced to commit and being powerless to stop them.

The worst part was knowing that this was only the beginning.

There was so much death and despair to come. I couldn't bear the thought of watching my own hand take so many lives.

It was time to face what I'd known all along—that fighting off Samael's hold was impossible.

It was time to give in.

And so, I sank deep into my soul, fading into darkness and allowing him to take over completely.

30

ANNIKA

THE GIRLS FOUND Jacen and I some fresh clothing, and we'd just finished changing when we heard the cacophony of howls.

Fear rushed through my body. The wolves were here. And from their angry howls, they were ready for war.

"You need to take cover," I told the girls. "Gather everyone else who stayed in the Tavern, and go somewhere safe."

"Where?" Fear shined in Laura's eyes, and she and the others watched me expectantly.

Her question gutted me, because I had no answer. Nowhere in the village would be safe from the wolves.

But they were scared enough as it was. I couldn't tell them that.

Still, I had to say *something.*

"Close all the windows and lock all the doors." I tried to sound confident, despite how much I feared for their lives. "Then bring everyone upstairs and stay as still and as quiet as you can."

It wasn't much—and I knew it wouldn't be enough—but I still prayed they'd be okay.

"What are you going to do?" Jill asked.

"There are witches in the palace," Jacen said. "We need to get to them and have one of them use a tracking spell to find Marigold."

"Wait." Jill focused on Jacen, her eyes apprehensive.

"What?" he asked.

"You don't have a weapon," she said. "You have two sheaths, but no weapon."

I glanced at the empty sheaths—they'd used to hold the daggers he'd used to blind the sea creature. But the daggers had sunk along with the creature and the rest of the boat.

"There are plenty of weapons in the palace," he said. "I'll find more there."

"Perhaps," she said. "But just in case something happens…" She hurried over to a bed and reached under the mattress, pulling out a gleaming dagger. "Here." She held it out to him. "This belonged to one of the girls who left. You should have it now."

"Thank you." Jacen accepted the dagger and placed it one of his sheaths. "I promise to repay this kindness."

"Repay it by stopping the wolves." Jill's voice was strong as she re-joined the other girls. They looked terrified, but as much as I wanted to comfort them, we couldn't stay here any longer.

"I'll transport us to the palace," I said, taking Jacen's hands in mine.

He nodded for me to go ahead, and I closed my eyes, imagining the palace and thinking about how much I wanted to bring us there.

The ground dropped from under me, and my stomach fell. Just like last time, the floor reappeared beneath us in seconds.

I opened my eyes and found us back inside the attic of the Tavern.

"What?" I looked around in frustration. "I was picturing the palace."

"Try again," Jacen said.

I did, but this time, we didn't even move.

"It's not working." I cursed myself for not having had more time to practice using my new abilities.

"Are you sure?" he asked.

"I'm sure," I said. "It's like I'm anchored to this place in the Vale."

"So I guess we'll just have to get to the palace the old

fashioned way." He was standing by the window before I could blink.

"Which way do you mean?" I asked.

He smirked, looking more than ready to take on whatever this upcoming fight would throw at him. "We'll run."

He jumped out of the window, and I rushed over to it, following his lead.

ANNIKA

THE HUMANS who remained in the village wandered into the streets in panic.

I wanted to stop them, tell them what I'd told the girls in the Tavern, and personally help get them to safety. But I didn't have time for that. Instead, I yelled instructions as Jacen and I ran down the streets, hoping that as many of them as possible would hear me and listen.

Soon, we crossed from the human village to the vampire town. The streets were empty compared to the human village, and I wondered if more vampires had gone with Alexander than we'd initially thought.

More likely, their enhanced hearing had allowed them to hear my instructions that I'd been screaming in the village. Hopefully, they'd listened.

We ran a few streets up toward the palace, making sure to keep in the alleys. That was when we saw the first bodies. There were only a few of them, but it was a gruesome sight—mangled limbs, heads ripped off at the neck from the wolves' teeth, and blood pooling on the streets.

Suddenly, I smelled the woodsy scent of wolf.

Both Jacen and I stopped in our tracks.

My hand was at my sword at the same time as the wolves appeared at both ends of the alley. There were only two of them, but they had us cornered.

Jacen and I stood with our backs together and weapons out, ready to fight.

"We're not your enemies." I stared down the wolf ahead of me, hoping to help them see reason before this turned ugly. The creature was still—although still on guard—so I continued. "My companion is a vampire, but I'm not. I'm an angel. And I'm here to tell you that the witch named Marigold has tricked you. She told you that your Savior is coming to help you, but she's lying. There *is* no Savior. She's possessed by a demon named Samael who's using you to help him open a Gate to Hell."

The wolves growled—I took that to mean that they didn't like what I had to say.

They ran toward us and were on us in seconds.

I took on one and Jacen took on the other. I wanted to turn around and make sure he was okay—after all, he only had one dagger to protect himself—but I had my own wolf to beat.

My wolf kept trying to jump around my sword to go for my neck, but I moved out of its path each time. The wolf was fast, but I was faster. I was also nimbler.

If we kept this up, I had no doubt that the wolf would soon tire and I'd be able to get in an easier blow.

"I don't want to kill you!" I said between breaths. "Look at my eyes—they're gold. I'm an angel. I'm telling you the truth."

The wolf only growled and ran for me again, although there was less force behind its pounce.

I moved out of the way, but pain slashed across my arm—the wolf's claw. I saw my golden blood in the corner of my eye. I wanted to reach for the wound, but I knew better than that—I had to stay on guard. Plus, it was already nearly healed.

The wolf circled me, studying me—more specifically, studying my eyes.

A whimper and the ploof of someone falling to the ground sounded from the other side of the alley.

The wolf I was fighting stopped in place, its eyes wide as it looked behind me.

I used the moment to tackle the wolf to the ground,

my knife at its throat. A quick glance behind me showed that Jacen was safe—he'd thrown his dagger straight into the heart of the wolf he'd been fighting—but I turned back to the wolf I was holding down, not wanting to give it a chance to escape.

"I don't want to kill you," I repeated, slower and calmer this time. "But I need you to listen to me."

The wolf shook underneath me. In our current position, I could see she was female, and she was clearly scared. She was making no move to fight back. It was almost like when Jacen had killed the wolf she'd been with, something had broken in her.

She glared at me, which I took to mean she was listening.

"I just want to find out where Marigold is," I continued. "Like I said, she's possessed by a demon named Samael, and to open the Hell Gate, Samael needs to be on a mountain soaked with the blood of supernaturals. He's gotten into your minds—he used Marigold's magic to plant the visions into your heads about your Savior— and he's turned you against the vampires so you'll do his dirty work for him. But the vampires and wolves need to work together to stop him. Samael *can't* be allowed to open the Hell Gate. If he does… the demons will come to Earth and destroy it."

Suddenly, the shape of the wolf blurred. Fur became

skin, and she shifted into human form right under my grip.

Holding onto her was impossible.

Jacen whizzed around to the other side of her, his knife up and ready.

But she was vulnerable while shifting, and I pounced on her before the shift was complete. I grabbed onto her arm, using my weight to pin her back down to the ground.

I was looking straight into the terrified eyes of a blonde girl who looked to be around my age. I was also relieved to find that she was fully clothed in what appeared to be animal pelts—apparently wolves were able to keep their clothes on while shifting.

She squirmed, and I tightened my grip on her arm, refusing to let her go.

"Are you ready to tell me where Marigold is?" I kept my blade pressed to her neck, hoping to show her that I meant business.

She glanced behind me—presumably at the other wolf's corpse—her eyes shining with tears. "If I do, will you let me live?" she asked.

"I will," I said. "As long as you make a blood oath with me that once our conversation is over, you'll leave the vampires' land and will tell no one of our conversation until the end of this war."

"Fine." She narrowed her eyes. "But only if *you* make a blood oath promising that everything you told me about Marigold and our Savior is the truth."

"Deal." The decision was easy—I *was* being honest with her, so I had no issue making the oath.

"Wait," she said, and I pressed my lips together, growing frustrated. Every moment we spent here was more time Marigold and the wolves had to slaughter the vampires.

I stared her down again, my silence a cue for her to continue.

"You said you're an angel," she said. "Do blood oaths even apply to angels?"

I wanted to tell her yes, but the truth was, I didn't know.

"They applied to me when I was a Nephilim—before I was turned into a full angel," I said. "That's all I know."

"I won't go against my pack for a blood oath that you don't even know will count," she said, and then she tilted her head slightly toward Jacen. "I want *him* to make the oath instead. The one who murdered my sister."

"This is war," Jacen said sharply. "I'm sorry for killing your sister. But if I hadn't, she would have killed me."

"And I would kill you for it if I didn't believe your girlfriend was telling the truth." The knife at her neck forced her to look at me as she spoke, but I could hear

145

the venom and hatred clearly enough in her tone to know that she meant it. "Your eyes could have been contacts, but I've never seen golden blood before."

I glanced down at where she'd scratched me—sure enough, my blood was smeared on my now-healed arm.

"I'll make the blood oath." Jacen stalked over to us and slashed his palm with his knife. Then he reached for the wolf-girl's other arm—the one I wasn't using to hold her down—and slashed her palm. He held her hand with his—blood against blood—and said, "I promise that everything Annika has told you regarding the demons and your Savior was the truth. In return, do you swear to truthfully tell us where to find Marigold, and then to leave the vampires' land and tell no one of what happened here until the war is over?"

"I swear," she said.

Jacen pulled his hand out of hers and stood up.

Both of their wounds were healed. The blood oath was complete.

I let up the pressure on the knife at her throat, although I didn't pull away completely. My instinct told me to trust the girl, but I couldn't risk anything until she followed through with her end of the oath.

"Marigold's holding back beyond the fighting," she said. "She's at the top of the tallest mountain peak inside the Vale, right outside a caved in cavern."

"The Crystal Cavern," I realized.

"Yes." The girl nodded. "That's what she called it."

"How many guards does she have with her?" Jacen asked.

"Only two," she answered. "She said there was no reason anyone would think to go there, and she wanted to send as many wolves into town as possible. We're supposed to go to her once every last vampire is dead."

"And the humans?" I asked.

"She doesn't care about the humans," she said. "We're supposed to ignore them until the vampires are taken care of. Then, if any of the humans cause trouble, we're to kill them afterward."

I breathed a sigh of relief that the humans who'd listened to my advice might end up being okay.

Well... they'd be okay if we stopped Marigold from opening the Hell Gate.

"Thank you for trusting me and helping me." I lifted my knife from the girl's neck, confident that she was no longer a threat. "What's your name?"

"Catie." The girl—Catie—stood up and reached for her neck as if checking to make sure she was still alive.

"Go," Jacen told her. "We're going to do everything we can to stop Marigold, but if we fail and the Hell Gate opens..." He paused, and Catie nodded, apparently not needing to hear any more.

She looked over at her sister one last time and kneeled down next to her fallen corpse. Her sister remained in wolf form—the form she'd been in when she'd died. "I'll come back for you," she promised.

Then she stood up, a cry escaping her throat before she turned around and ran out of town.

32

KARINA

WHILE MOST OF the pack was attacking the vampire town, I led Noah and a group of thirty wolves around the edge of the boundary and toward the back of the palace. The sun had fully risen by now, and it was burning down upon my skin. I needed to get inside before I became too weak to fight.

The windows in the palace were made of hurricane-proof glass—they were impossible to shatter, even by supernaturals. But I'd left the window to the quarters where I'd stayed during Prince Jacen's selection unlocked.

I was praying that the staff hadn't noticed and re-locked it between then and now.

While staying in the palace in the Vale, I'd been amazed by how easy it had been to sneak in and out at my will. The vampires of the Vale were so confident in their witch's ability to maintain the boundary, and so sure of the peace treaty they had with the wolves, that they hadn't bothered to make the palace as secure as possible.

Unlike the fort-like castle in the Carpathian Kingdom, the palace in the Vale had been built for beauty, not for war.

"Once the path is clear, I'll throw the rope," I told Noah.

He was in his wolf form—as were the others—but he nodded in acknowledgment.

I made sure my backpack was secured in place. Then I jumped up to the window that had been my quarters, situated myself on the sill, and pushed on the glass.

It didn't budge.

"Shit," I said, banging my fists against the glass. It wouldn't shatter—the glass was too strong—but it helped get out my frustration.

I banged on it a few more times, screaming profanities and ready to give up and jump back down to join the wolves.

Then there was a movement from inside.

Daisy—the young vampire who had cleaned my quarters when I'd stayed at the Vale—crawled out from under the bed. Her eyes widened when she saw me, and she hurried to the window to unlock it.

"Princess Karina!" She smiled, opening the window to let me inside. "I thought it sounded like you. I didn't want to come out when I heard the banging, but then I heard your voice. I've been so worried ever since hearing that you disappeared from the palace! Where have you been this entire time?"

I scooted inside, my heart dropping as she spoke.

The poor girl didn't realize that we weren't on the same side.

"Where are Prince Scott and Princess Stephenie?" I asked, since I was unable to answer any of her questions —at least without my answers being lies.

"They're in the throne room," she said. "It's the safest room in the palace. You should go there, too."

"Why aren't you there?" I asked.

"No staff allowed." She shrugged. "Only royal vampires and their guards."

She went to re-lock the window, but I reached for her, stopping her.

"What?" she asked. "We can't leave any of the windows unlocked. Not when the wolves are so close."

"I've brought others with me."

Daisy's smile brightened. "Has the Carpathian

Kingdom come to fight for the Vale?" she asked. "Have you come to save us?"

As I led her away from the open window, guilt wracked my chest at how much she trusted me. I *hated* turning on my own species. Especially when so many of them were innocents like Daisy.

But Daisy had let me in—maybe the wolves wouldn't kill her. Perhaps I could convince them to let her go. She'd need to leave the Vale—no more vampires could remain on this land for the Savior to rise—but maybe she could still join Prince Alexander.

How could she possibly get to him? What used to be the vampire boundary was surrounded by wolves. If she ran, she'd be killed.

There had to be *something* I could do...

"They're waiting for my signal," I told her. "But I don't want them to see you. Can you hide under the bed again?"

"Why can't they see me?" she asked.

"They might want you to help fight," I said the first lie that popped into my mind. "And you don't know how to fight, do you?"

"No." She hung her head, looking ashamed. "I don't."

"That's what I thought." I motioned to under the bed. "Go. Quickly."

She didn't look convinced, but she still lowered herself to the floor, scooting back underneath the bed.

I fixed up the bed skirt, flattening it so no one would be able to tell that it had just been messed with. Once satisfied, I placed my backpack down and unzipped it, pulling out a long rope.

Wolves couldn't jump as high as vampires, which was why the back of the palace had been unguarded. Naturally, Scott had placed all of the guards at the location the wolves *could* get in from—the main entrance. Why waste the limited guards they had on the back when it was impossible for the wolves to not only jump so high, but also impossible for supernaturals to break the glass?

I looked down at the rope in my hands and took a deep breath. After all my decades of living, I never imagined I would have ended up here.

But one glance back down at the wolves—at Noah—reminded me what I was fighting for. This wasn't just *a* pack—it was *my* pack.

Plus, if I didn't help them now, I would surely die.

I headed to the window and tossed the rope down, holding the end to keep it supported.

Noah was the first to shift into his human form and climb up. Once inside, he looked around, his eyes bulging as he took in the extravagance of the room. I couldn't blame him—the canopied bed, carved wooden furniture, Turkish rug, and crystal chandelier were a different world from his rugged tent at camp.

"This is where you lived?" he asked, his mouth dropping open in shock.

"This was where I stayed as a visiting princess to the Vale." I lifted my chin, purposefully trying to sound as snobbish as possible in an attempt to make a joke of it. "You should have seen my quarters in the Carpathian Kingdom. Or maybe not—King Nicolae wouldn't be too happy to have a wolf drooling on his floor."

Noah closed his mouth, returning once more to the fierce fighter I knew. "The Savior better bring all the prosperity He promised, because we have a lot to live up to," he said.

"I'm sure he will," I said, mainly because I *hoped* he would.

It was hard enough to imagine living with a pack of wolves, let alone living in a *camp*. I had to consciously keep myself from shuddering at the thought.

"Where'd the vampire go?" he asked. "The one who let you in?"

"I compelled her to return to her room and forget she saw me." The guilt in my chest grew as I lied to Noah.

"Why didn't you take care of her yourself?"

"I couldn't." I lowered my eyes, glad that at least I didn't have to lie this time. "I knew her when I was staying at the Vale—she's innocent and kind. I was hoping that maybe, if there's a way we could figure out to get her to Prince Alexander, she could be spared. After all, she helped me by opening the window, and she told me where Prince Scott and Princess Stephenie are."

"She helped you because she thought you were on her side." He placed a finger under my chin and lifted my eyes back up to meet his. "Do you think she would have helped if she knew where your allegiances truly lie?"

"No." It took all of my self-control to resist glancing at the bed to make sure she wasn't going to give away her location. Instead, I focused on Noah's eyes—his deep, trusting eyes.

I wished I could believe as strongly as he did that the vampires of the Vale needed to die. But I didn't.

And it was too late to turn back now.

"The others are waiting." Noah pulled away from me and faced the window. "Where are the prince and princess?"

"In the throne room," I answered. "I can lead us there."

He gave the others a thumbs up and held the rope steady.

One by one, the wolves climbed through the window to join us. Soon, they were all up—each one of them was as amazed with the luxurious quarters as Noah had been. They still hadn't shifted back to wolf form, and many of them were wandering around, touching and examining everything they could.

"Prince Scott and Princess Stephenie are in the throne room," Noah said, making eye contact with as many wolves as he could. "We need to go there at once. Princess Karina will lead us. Kill all the vampires who get in our way."

"Wait." A wolf examining the carved canopy bed paused and gave a long, deep sniff. "I smell vampire."

33

KARINA

MY BREATH CAUGHT at the realization that he'd smelled Daisy. The wolves' sense of smell wasn't as heightened in human form—I'd been hoping they wouldn't be able to tell her scent from mine.

"You smell me." I rolled my eyes, as if he were being ridiculous. "Or am I already so accepted into the pack that you've forgotten I'm a vampire?"

He eyed up the bed and kneeled down, sniffing near the bottom of it. "It's not you I smell," he said, and then he reached for the bed skirt, pulling it up. "It's *her*."

He and the wolf next to him reached under the bed and dragged out Daisy, each of them holding onto one of her arms. She was kicking and screaming, and she looked at me with wild, terrified eyes. She didn't have to speak for me to know what she was thinking.

How could you have betrayed your own kind?

One of the other wolves broke the rod holding up the canopied bed and shoved the makeshift stake through Daisy's heart.

She dropped to the floor, dead.

"You knew she was there." The wolf that had killed Daisy glared at me while pointing at her corpse. "You betrayed us."

I opened my mouth to speak, but no words came.

"Karina didn't betray us." Noah stepped in front of me and held his arms out, protecting me. "She let me know the girl was hiding there before you all came up. That girl was the informant who'd told us the whereabouts of Prince Scott and Princess Stephenie. She'd been compelled to stay there and say nothing until we returned to take care of her." He glanced at Daisy's corpse in irritation. "Which would have been much quieter than the ruckus you caused just now. Were you trying to let every vampire in the palace know we're here?"

I stepped up to Noah's side and gave him a single nod, hoping he could see the gratefulness in my eyes. Then I turned to the men. "As it is now, we have no time to waste," I said, quickly jumping back into the role of leader of the pack. "Once we reach the throne room, wait for my command to kill the prince and princess. As royal vampires, they deserve to know what they're dying for."

A few of the wolves mumbled words that I didn't quite pick up.

"Did you all hear the princess?" Noah asked, glaring at them.

"Yes." They stood at attention when their First Prophet spoke.

"Will you do as she requests?"

"Yes," they said, although many didn't look happy to say it.

"Good." I tried to ignore the sinking feeling in my gut that after this war was over, I might never be able to live with myself. "Shift—now. I'll lead you to the throne room."

The wolves did as I commanded, and I took one last regretful look at Daisy's still body before flinging open the doors and sprinting down the hall.

34

KARINA

THE WOLVES TORE through any vampires who got in our way. Like expected, there weren't many vampire guards stationed *inside* the palace. They were mostly outside, guarding the entrance.

Despite having my sword at my side, I had yet to use it to fight. The wolves were able to attack the vampires quickly enough that I didn't need to.

I had yet to kill *any* vampires during this war.

At least the wolves were strong enough fighters to do the dirty work for me. And luckily, most of the vampire nobles and staff had the common sense to stay inside their rooms. But hiding wouldn't buy them much time. Because after taking care of the royals, the wolves were coming for every last vampire in the palace.

This was only the beginning of the bloodshed to come.

Finally, after leaving corpses of vampire guards in our wake, we approached the double-door entrance to the throne room. The room was located deep inside the palace—if I hadn't sneaked the wolves inside through the back, it would have been *much* harder to reach.

I pushed open the door, finding Scott and Stephenie sitting on the two thrones. They wore their crowns on their heads and were dressed like they were ready for a fancy ball—Scott in a tuxedo and Stephenie in a radiant red gown.

They weren't waiting to fight.

They were waiting to die.

Shock registered on their faces when they saw me. I must have looked quite the sight as I entered with a pack of wolves on my heels.

I held my hands down, and as requested, the wolves refrained from attacking. But I could hear their snarls behind me—they were ready to kill.

"Princess Karina," Scott said in disdain. "When you ran off after Queen Laila's death, we assumed you'd returned to the Carpathian Kingdom. But if you'd returned, you would have told King Nicolae of the queen's death, and he would have been enraged. When we didn't hear from him, we asked around and learned you'd been spotted at the Haven. It seemed unlikely that you'd chosen to live such a modest life there, but I could accept it as true. However, I must admit that this—you working with these *animals*—is quite the shock."

"Especially since you hate the wolves," Stephenie spat. "The shifters killed the love of your life. Now you're *working* with them. You're even more disgusting than they are."

I flinched at the mention of the love of my life—she must be referring to the "Peter" that Noah had told me about.

But I couldn't let myself think about the man I didn't remember. Right now, I could only think about the facts of why I was here.

"Prince Alexander told both of you about the wolves' visions of their Savior—he told all the citizens of the Vale," I said. "He told you that if you didn't leave, you would die. Yet, you remain here. Why?"

Scott turned his nose up at me. "I can't explain loyalty to someone who has none," he said, his eyes empty and cold. "Right, sister?"

Stephenie frowned, refusing to look at her brother. "No." She sounded small and meek, despite her fancy gown and jewels. "Princess Karina may not be right in turning on her own kind, but you weren't right in staying here, either. We should have gone with our brother. I didn't go with him because I was afraid. But Alexander was right—it's better to fear an uncertain future than to have no future at all."

I took a sharp breath inward, not having expected her to say that.

Scott stood from his throne to tower in front of Stephenie. "*What* was that?" he seethed, his hand wrapped around the hilt of his sword.

"We should have gone with Alexander." She stared up at him defiantly. "More than that, we should have made Alexander the acting king—not you. Maybe if he'd been king, we wouldn't be about to be ripped apart by wild animals."

"Oh, don't worry, sister," he said. "I have no intention of letting you be ripped apart by animals."

He raised his sword and ran it through her heart, pinning her to the back of her throne.

The princess's eyes glazed over, but she remained upright, her tiara still balanced perfectly on her head.

Even in death, Stephenie was beautiful.

Scott stepped away, although he left his sword where it was, sliced straight through his sister's chest. "Well?" He turned to face me, raising an eyebrow. "Are you just going to stand there, or are you going to tell your dogs to rip my head off?"

I didn't bother giving the wolves the signal.

Instead, I rushed for Scott and raised my sword, getting a clean strike through his neck.

His head rolled to the ground, his body crumpling to the floor.

I don't know how long I stood there staring at him before someone took my hand in his. Noah.

"You're shaking," he said, pulling me toward him.

"You need to shift back to your wolf form," I said, still staring at Scott's remains. "You can defend yourself best in your wolf form."

"We've taken down all the guards in the palace." He raised his hand to my face and forced me to look at him, his eyes deep and caring as he gazed into mine. "The vampires that remain are all cowering in their rooms, so there's no more immediate threat. Right now, you need me—in my *human* form."

His lowered his lips to mine, and I melted into his kiss, squeezing my eyes shut and pulling him closer. I didn't care that the other wolves were watching. I just kissed Noah like his touch could erase the horrors I'd helped create.

It didn't help. I wanted it to, but I felt nothing.

I felt empty.

What had I done?

35

ANNIKA

"To get to the mountain, we'll have to go through all the fighting in town," Jacen said. "It would be much faster if you could teleport us there."

"I can try," I said, although after my failed attempt to bring us to the palace, I wasn't sure.

"A wise man once said—do or do not, there is no try."

"Did you just quote Star Wars?" I chuckled, although my heart panged at the memory of my brother. Grant used to quote that exact same line.

"You bet I did." He stepped closer and took my hands in his. "Now, are you ready to *do* this?"

"I am," I said. "But there's no place to hide at the top of the mountain. The moment we get there, we need to be ready to fight. Any delay could cost us our lives."

"Got it." Jacen watched me intently, waiting for me to bring us there.

I took a deep breath, not feeling ready in the slightest. Everything since the moment I'd killed Laila had happened so quickly that I'd barely had time to process what I was about to do. I was about to kill a *demon*.

How could someone ever feel ready for that?

Then I remembered what Rosella and Emmanuel had told me—this was my destiny. If a psychic vampire and an angel believed in me, then I *must* be able to do this. Plus, if I didn't do this, the whole world would be at the mercy of the demons.

I *refused* to let that happen.

I pictured the top of the mountain—I'd only been there once, when Camelia had taken me to retrieve Geneva's sapphire ring. The peak was above the tree line, so it was just a gaping cave amongst an endless amount of snow. I thought about how I wanted to transport us straight there, and how I couldn't mess up—getting us there could mean the end of this war.

My stomach dropped—I didn't think I'd ever be able to get used to the sensation of teleporting—and the air around me became colder, the ground softer. Snow.

I opened my eyes and saw two wolves running toward us. But we readied our weapons, and in seconds, the wolves were dead at our feet, the snow turning red from their blood.

Slow clapping echoed from nearby.

I spun around and saw a pale, frail girl with delicate features and long brown hair. She looked like a young teen. She wore the same animal pelt clothing as the wolves, and had a sword and dagger strapped to her sides.

But she didn't move to attack. She just tilted her head and gave us a close-lipped smile.

"Samael," I said, since I was truly speaking to the demon possessing her—not to the girl she truly was.

"What?" Confusion passed over her features—if I didn't know better, I would have believed that she didn't know what I was talking about. "My name is Marigold."

"That might be Marigold's body, but you're Samael," I said. "Emmanuel told me all about you before sending me here to end you. The game is up. It's time for you to raise your sword and fight."

Her lower lip trembled, and she reached for her sword, clumsily pulling it out of its sheath. "I'm only a witch." She held the sword with both hands, her arms shaking. "I don't know how to fight."

"Save it," I said, and I ran at her, using my sword to knock hers out of her hands.

She fell to the ground and looked up at me in terror.

I raised my sword, ready to kill her.

Except that as I stood there, staring down at the helpless, shivering girl, I couldn't. Yes, I knew it was an act—that Samael was controlling her and using her innocence to guilt me into not killing her. But Marigold was still in there. She'd never asked to be possessed by a demon. She was innocent—and she was so *young*. She should have her whole life ahead of her.

She reminded me of myself a little over a year ago— when I'd been a helpless human at the mercy of the vampires who had kidnapped me to the Vale. Killing her like this—when she wasn't fighting back—would be cold-blooded, heartless murder.

She remained where she was, stark still in the snow, and started muttering under her breath.

"What?" I leaned closer to make out what she was saying.

She just smiled, reached for her dagger, and slashed it across her neck.

"No!" I dropped my sword and kneeled down next to her, pressing my hands against the wound to try stopping the blood.

But there was *so much* blood. It flowed and flowed, staining her clothes and the snow around her. Soon we were sitting in a puddle of it.

Her breaths rattled, and she moved her lips, but she

couldn't speak. Instead, she gave me one last smile. Then her head lolled back, her eyes glazing over.

Dead.

Suddenly, an explosion sounded from the vampire town.

A well of blackness opened up, reaching up past the clouds. A shadow fell over the sun, making it look like night. It was so dark that the crickets started chirping and an owl hooted nearby.

Gray shadows swirled up and out of the darkness. Wild, storming wind ripped through the air, and a chill traveled down to my bones.

"The Hell Gate," I said, horror shaking me to the core as I stared out at the black void. "It's open."

ANNIKA

JACEN RUSHED to me and pulled me away from Marigold's body.

I hadn't even remembered that I'd been holding her until she thumped to the ground. I was barely even aware of Jacen's arms around me.

All I could see were the demons bursting out of the Hell Gate.

"Marigold's blood," Jacen said, looking down at the ground in horror.

"What?" My eyes shot to his—how could he be struggling with bloodlust at a time like this?

"Look at it," he said, and I did.

Wisps of smoke rose from the puddle of her blood. The blood itself was also changing color—from red to black.

One of the gray shapes from the Hell Gate fell next to the blood. It was the size of a human—a very large human—and it materialized into a strong, tall man with dark brown hair and chiseled features.

He would have been handsome if he didn't radiate evil.

He took a deep breath in, and the smoke from Marigold's blood entered his mouth and nose. Once the final wisps disappeared inside of him, his eyes glowed red, and he smiled. His teeth were long and pointy—revulsion passed through me at the sight of them.

"Damn." He brought his hands together behind his back and cracked his spine, finishing it off with a final crack of his neck. "It feels good to have my body back."

"Samael," I said his name darkly, the pit of despair in my chest growing larger with each second.

"In the flesh." He kicked Marigold's corpse, sending it up and over the side of the mountain. "I traded up from that pathetic little witch, don't you think? Actually, I don't care what you think, since you—*and* your vampire boyfriend—are about to die."

I narrowed my eyes at him and dove for my sword, but I wasn't fast enough—Samael got it first.

He brought it down toward me, but I rolled away before it could slice me in two. It cut into the ground instead.

"Dammit!" he said, yanking the sword from the ground.

Before he had a chance to swing again, Jacen was on him. He'd somehow gotten ahold of Marigold's sword and was using it to hold Samael off.

Which left only one available weapon nearby— Marigold's dagger.

The dagger she'd used to slice her throat and open the Hell Gate.

I took the dagger and glanced back over at Jacen and Samael. Samael was larger than even Jacen, and the two of them were engrossed in a dangerous dance of sword fighting. They moved so fast that they would have been blurs to the human eye, but my angel sight could keep up with them just fine.

Jacen was slowing down, but Samael looked just as energized as ever.

I needed to do something. Now.

I ran with the dagger in hand, ramming it straight through Samael's back and into his heart.

He froze, and I let go of the handle, taking a step back.

I'd done it. I'd had to stab him in the back, but what did it matter *how* I'd killed him?

All that mattered was that he was dead.

But he delivered a blow to Jacen's face that knocked

him across the clearing, and he spun around to face me. His red eyes glowed, and he flashed me a creepy lopsided smile. "You *really* shouldn't have done that," he said.

Then he pulled the dagger out of his back and threw it straight at me.

I dashed out of the way, but the blade clipped the side of my arm, and I screamed.

"Angel blood." Samael took a deep breath in, smiled again, and licked his lips. "It always smells as fresh as the Garden of Eden. Especially baby angel blood." He laughed, the emptiness of it sending shivers down my spine, and set the tip of the sword into the ground. He put some of his weight on it, standing there like a perverse circus ringleader. "What was Emmanuel thinking, sending a baby angel to kill *me*?" he asked, laughing again. "He must be desperate."

At the mention of Emmanuel, I remembered the last part of what he'd told me up in Heaven, when he was instructing me on how to kill Samael.

Demons couldn't be killed with a regular sword.

I needed a sword that had been dipped in heavenly water. More specifically, I needed *my* sword that Emmanuel had dipped in the heavenly cloud.

The sword that Samael was currently holding.

It wasn't going to be easy. But I had one advantage—

Samael clearly underestimated me. Of course he did, after seeing how I hadn't been able to kill Marigold. He thought I was weak. A "*baby* angel."

I would show him.

And so, I stared at the spot right next to Samael, thinking about how much I wanted to be there instead of where I was currently standing across from him. I didn't bother closing my eyes this time—I needed to be alert and ready.

My stomach dropped, the world blurred around me, and a second later, I was next to Samael.

I kicked the sword to knock it out of his hand, caught it in mine, and rammed it through his heart.

His eyes met mine, and he disintegrated into ashes.

Well, *mostly* into ashes. The only things remaining in the pile were his pointed, disgusting demon teeth.

I plucked one of them of the ashes and shoved it into my pocket.

"Why'd you take that?" Jacen stepped up next to me, glancing down at the teeth at our feet.

"Proof that we killed him," I said. "Not that it matters, since we failed." I gazed out at the open Hell Gate, hopelessness sinking into my bones once more.

Wherever the demons were going, I had no doubt that they would bring evil and darkness in their wake.

At the thought of darkness, Rosella's prophecy

echoed in my mind. *No matter what, we'll end up with a different world—a dark world. But your decisions will determine how dark it'll get.*

Was this what she'd meant? Had the Hell Gate always been fated to open, no matter what I'd chosen to do?

The part about my decisions was the only thing giving me hope. Or perhaps that part had already come to pass when I'd been unable to kill Marigold.

I'd had an important decision to make, and I'd chosen wrong.

Now the entire world would pay for my mistake.

"Maybe we didn't fail." Jacen's voice pulled me out of my grim thoughts.

"The Hell Gate is open," I said. "How can we possibly fix this?"

"I don't know," he said, and he took my hand, pulling me toward the Hell Gate. "But we owe it to ourselves— and the world—to go over there and try."

CAMELIA

THE HAVEN PUT me in a guest room while they were getting my permanent accommodation ready. The room was simple, and I mostly stayed inside of it, contemplating all my recent decisions. I also prayed for the Vale. What I'd told Alexander had seemed to get through to him, and I hoped with all of my being that he'd led as many citizens to safety as he could.

Now, Mary led me through the luscious grounds of the Haven toward the cabin that would be my new home. The air here felt thicker and wetter than in the Vale, and there seemed to be a constant chorus of animals coming from the rain forest. I felt foreign—like an outsider who didn't belong.

I doubted I would ever get used to living here. How could this strange land ever feel like home?

But I rested my hand on my belly, the motion bringing me peace.

The safety of my child was more than worth this change.

We walked along a row of cabins, and my stomach sank in disappointment. While the cabins appeared sturdy and well maintained, they were so *small*.

Maybe these cabins were for the workers, and the larger accommodations were further out. That must be it. Surely a witch of my standing would be provided a larger living space than an average worker.

"Here we are." Mary stopped in front of a cabin that was the same size as all the others.

I hid the horror from my face as I followed her up the steps. I didn't want to seem ungrateful—after all, the Haven was doing me a courtesy by taking me in—but I also felt insulted.

I prayed there was a spell around the cabins—something that made the interiors larger than the outsides appeared.

Upon following Mary inside, it became apparent that there was no such spell. The inside of was just as confining as I'd dreaded. There weren't even separate rooms—the bed was in a nook that could see straight into the living room and tiny kitchen.

The few personal items that I'd brought in my suitcase had been placed on the kitchen counter.

"You can put your belongings wherever you'd like," Mary said. "The closets are filled with the uniform of the Haven, tailored to your size. The clothes you brought with you have been donated to charity, since you'll have no need for them here."

My throat went dry as I looked around the cabin. My clothes were some of the few things I'd had from my life. Now they'd been taken from me, without my permission.

As I looked around, I realized that this stark, confined space would *never* feel like home.

"You look ill," Mary observed. "Is everything all right?"

No, everything most certainly was *not* all right. She might as well have just told me that I'd be living in a dungeon—prison uniform and all.

But if I said that, she might kick me out of the Haven. Then I'd truly have no place to go.

I had to tread cautiously—both for my sake and my child's.

"Is this size cabin typical for citizens of the Haven?" I tried to phrase the question in the most inoffensive way possible.

"It is." Mary nodded. "All citizens who live alone are

provided a cabin of this size—including myself. Once your child is born, you'll be moved into a cabin suited for two."

"Oh." I studied her, her answer taking me by surprise. "You live in the same size cabin as everyone else?"

"I do." Her laugh was light and welcoming. "I'm sure it's a lot to get used to after the Vale. While I haven't been to the Vale myself, the witches who have gone there to fetch royals for diplomatic meetings have informed me of the splendor of your quarters. But splendor brings trouble as well—mainly, that many are given far less than what they need to balance it out. Here at the Haven, everyone is equal. But we look out for our own. So if there's ever anything you need, just come to me and if the request is in reason, I'll do my best to be of service."

"Thank you," I said, meaning it.

Living here was certainly going to be a lot to get used to. But I owed it to myself—and to my child —to try.

"There actually is one thing I need of help with, if you have time to listen," I said.

"Of course." She walked over to the couch, motioning for me to join her. "Come, sit."

I sat, glad to find that the couch—while plain—was

comfortable. "There's more to my pregnancy than I initially told you," I started, resting a hand on my stomach as I spoke.

"I had a feeling as much." She gave me a small smile, waiting for me to continue.

I was ready to tell her the full truth. But I'd also made a blood oath with Laila that I wouldn't tell anyone what she'd told me about how the original vampires went to the fae to become what they were. Blood oaths hold even past death.

I'd need to be cautious in my wording, but I could still tell Mary the most important part about how my child was conceived—the part that required her help.

"In order to locate Geneva's sapphire ring, I went to the fae," I began.

Mary frowned the moment I mentioned the word fae, but she made no judgements, simply waiting for me to continue.

"I called upon them and was met by a fae man named Prince Devyn," I said. "As a price for his passage from the Otherworld, he requested my first born child once he or she came of age. I'd previously made a deal with Laila that if I retrieved Geneva's sapphire ring for her, she'd turn me into a vampire. Since I wouldn't be able to have children as a vampire, I thought nothing of Prince Devyn's request. I agreed, thinking I'd been clever enough to get one over on the fae.

"From there, we made a deal that he would tell me who had Geneva's sapphire ring if I gave him something I'd never given to anyone before," I continued. "After a few questions, I agreed. He gave me the answers I wanted—he told me where to find Geneva's sapphire ring—and then he told me what he wanted from me."

"Your virginity," Mary said, glancing at my stomach.

I sat back in surprise, feeling stupid for falling into his trap after her being able to figure it out so quickly. "How did you know?" I asked.

"I've heard of Prince Devyn," Mary said. "All fae are blessed with a magical gift from birth, with some of those gifts being more powerful than others. He has one of the most powerful gifts in existence—omniscient sight."

"He does," I said, since he'd told me as much.

"The child growing in your womb is the result of your union with Prince Devyn," she continued, and I nodded, since of course she was correct. "Half-witch, half-fae. And that child is bound to join his or her father in the Otherworld once he or she comes of age."

"Yes." I leaned forward, calmed by how easily she was taking this in. Surely that meant she had a solution to my problem? "Once my child is born, he or she will be a citizen of the Haven. You said you'll do anything to give the citizens of the Haven what they need. My child needs to stay here where it's safe—not to be taken to the Otherworld. Is there anything you can do to help us?"

Mary glanced out of the window, and then turned back to me. "I can provide a safe place for you and your child to live until he or she comes of age," she said. "You'll both be comfortable and out of danger in the Haven."

"But what about after coming of age?" I asked. "I can't let my child be taken to the Otherworld."

"You made a deal with the fae." Mary's eyes were sad —I assumed she was thinking about her own deal she'd made with the fae to give up all her mortal memories in exchange for becoming a vampire. "You're bound to that deal by magic more powerful than anyone in the Haven —by magic more powerful than anyone on *Earth*."

"So there's nothing you can do?" I sat back, stunned. Until now, I'd held onto hope that I could change my child's fate.

That hope was disappearing with each passing minute.

"I can provide a safe place for you to enjoy the time you have with your child before he or she comes of age," she said. "After that, the child belongs to the Otherworld."

"We have a while before my child comes of age," I said, not willing to give up that easily. "Surely we can find another—"

I was cut off by someone bursting into my cabin.

A vampire who'd been turned when she'd been a young teen stood in the doorframe, her milky eyes staring straight ahead.

She was blind.

"Rosella." Mary stood, looking more offended by the intrusion than I felt. "What on Earth—"

"A Hell Gate has opened in the Vale." The vampire—Rosella—spoke quickly and calmly. "Demons are escaping as we speak."

"What?" I gazed at Rosella, then at Mary, and then back to Rosella again. "Where did you hear this? How do you know it's true?"

"I'm a psychic." Rosella looked in my direction, although her milky gaze didn't focus *on* me. "What I say is true."

I nodded, believing her.

Then I realized she couldn't see me nod.

"What about the wolves' Savior?" I asked. "I thought He was going to rise and save the Vale."

"There was never any Savior," Rosella said. "The greater demon Samael was tricking the wolves the entire time. Annika and Jacen set out to kill Samael, but they were too late. Annika killed him, but only after he succeeded in opening the Hell Gate."

"We must go there." Determination flashed across Mary's eyes. "We need to close the Hell Gate."

"How?" I stood as well, fear rolling through my body as I thought about the horrors that must be happening to my home. "My magic is strong, but not *that* strong. It takes an entire *coven* to close a Hell Gate. And even then…"

I didn't continue, unable to bring myself to say it out loud. It had been over two millennia since a Hell Gate had been opened, but all supernaturals knew of the ultimate sacrifice given by the coven that had closed it.

To close the Hell Gate, they'd had to deplete their magic.

It had been their Final Spell.

Afterward, the angels had blessed the world with the only species capable of defeating the demons—the Nephilim. It took the Nephilim over a thousand years to kill all the escaped demons and send them back to Hell.

It was only *after* killing all the demons that the Nephilim had settled for new targets—vampires, witches, and shifters. That had ultimately led to the Great War and the destruction of all the known Nephilim on Earth.

"We won't need a coven." Mary sounded confident enough that I had a feeling she had a plan.

"Why not?" I asked.

"Because I have this."

She reached for a chain around her neck and pulled a pendant out from beneath her shirt—Geneva's sapphire ring.

CAMELIA

"WHAT?" I gasped. "You've had Geneva's sapphire ring this entire time?"

"I have," she said. "According to one of Rosella's prophecies, Annika could only take one person with her on her quest if she hoped to succeed. Annika chose to bring Prince Jacen, and she left Geneva in my indefinite care."

"She chose to bring a young vampire prince instead of the most powerful witch in the world who would do anything she commanded?" I rolled my eyes, amazed that the girl could be so daft.

"Annika made the correct choice," Rosella said. "Geneva didn't have Annika's best wishes at heart, and choosing Prince Jacen was instrumental in her success."

"And yet, the Hell Gate is still open," I said.

"Yes." She nodded. "The future is never set in stone, but I'm afraid that after Annika's powers were activated, the Hell Gate was always likely to open again soon. The question is—how long will it *stay* open?"

"So it can be closed?" I asked.

"Yes," she said. "And we'll all three want to go there to try. Specifically you, Camelia."

"Why?" My hand instinctively went to my stomach again. "I'm pregnant, and the Vale is a war zone. I can't risk losing the baby."

"Trust me." Rosella smiled. "You'll want to be there."

Before I could ask for more information, Mary rubbed the sapphire stone and Geneva materialized beside us. The witch looked the same as the first time I'd seen her in the Vale's throne room—like Cleopatra in a flapper dress.

She looked around the cabin and yawned. "You called?" She crossed her arms and looked at Mary, tapping her foot as she waited for an answer.

"A Hell Gate has been opened at the Vale." Mary was quick to get to the point. "Can you close it?"

"I don't know." Geneva sounded as blasé as ever—as if she were asked to close Hell Gates all the time. "As I'm sure you know, the most recent Hell Gate was closed long before I was born."

"Right," Mary said. "I should have known you'd be

difficult. So, I command you to transport me, Rosella, Camelia, and two of my tiger shifters to the Vale, where you'll do everything in your power to try and close the Hell Gate."

39

GENEVA

I DID AS MARY COMMANDED—IT wasn't like I had a choice.

We landed in the main square in town… or at least what *used* to be the main square in town.

Right in the center of the square was a never-ending black pit, with darkness rising up from it and all the way up above the clouds. Wind howled from the pit as gray, spirit-like creatures rose from it—demons. Wolves gathered around the opening in their human forms, kneeling as if bowed down in prayer. The streets were littered with corpses—mostly vampires, but wolves as well. The buildings were cracked and lopsided, like they'd been through an earthquake.

Just looking at the darkness rising from the ground sent despair through my body. This felt more hopeless than when I'd been locked inside that wretched sapphire ring.

There was only one time in my life when I'd felt a horror worse than this—when I'd been called from my ring in the throne room and had seen the pile of ashes that had once been Laila.

Trusting that I'd see Laila again was all that had kept me sane when I'd been locked inside that sapphire prison. She'd been the only person who had ever understood and loved me, as I'd been the only person who had ever understood and truly loved her. We were meant to be.

When the witches had locked me in that ring, they hadn't realized that they were giving me what I'd always wanted—immortality while being able to keep my powers.

Once Laila had command over the ring, we would have finally been able to be together forever.

With her gone, I had nothing.

Suddenly, two figures materialized across the way— Prince Jacen and Annika.

Hatred rushed through me at the sight of the girl who had killed my soul mate.

Annika held onto Jacen's hand, and I hated her even more for having someone after she'd taken Laila from me. I curled my hands into fists, wanting to unleash all the darkest magic I could find straight at her and make her hurt even *half* as much as she'd hurt me.

But of course, I couldn't.

I could only use my magic when my owner commanded me to do so.

"This is all your fault." I snarled at Annika. If looks could kill, she'd be dead right now. "If Laila were alive, this never would have happened."

"That's not true," someone said from next to me—the blind vampire prophet, Rosella. "This was all going to happen whether Laila was alive or not. In fact, when Annika killed Laila and ignited her Nephilim powers, she made everything *better*, not worse."

"Shut up," I snapped, not wanting to hear it. I should have left her back at the Haven so I wouldn't have to listen to her prattling on about Annika's virtues.

Except of course I couldn't, because I'd been commanded by Mary to bring her here.

"Stop bickering." Mary stepped between us, although she remained focused on me. "Every moment the Hell Gate remains open, more demons escape. I command you to close it. Now."

I stepped forward and peered down into the void, watching the gray demon souls shoot out of the opening.

Looking into the Hell Gate, I knew what I'd known

since learning of its opening—my magic wasn't strong enough to fix this. My magic was as close to infinite as any witch's that had ever lived, but I was no god. Even I had my limits.

There was only one way I could close the Hell Gate —by depleting my magic.

Closing the Hell Gate would be my Final Spell.

The power of a Final Spell was that it was a sacrifice a witch *chose* to give. Not even the witches who had locked me inside the sapphire ring could take that choice away from me.

That choice had always existed—I'd simply never wanted to use it until now.

It was ironic, really. I'd longed for immortality the entire time I'd been mortal, as it was the only way Laila and I could be together forever without me becoming a vampire. Now I finally had immortality. But with Laila gone, immortality was a curse—not a gift.

I didn't want to live in a world without Laila.

She was in the Beyond, and the one thing I wished for above all else was to be there with her. No one knew what waited in the Beyond, but both Laila and I had done enough horrible things during our years that I doubted what waited for us would be anything good.

Maybe if my Final Spell saved the world, my sins would be forgiven. Maybe it would negate every awful thing I'd done and I'd get my wish to be with Laila forever.

With that hope in mind, I held my hands out, pressing my palms against the edge of the darkness that rose from Hell. Despair filled me upon touching it, but I gathered my magic within myself and focused on my goal. The magic grew and grew until it filled up my entire body so much that I felt like I was glowing with it.

When I touched the darkness, it started to dissolve. Not a lot—not enough to dissolve completely—but enough that I knew that my magic was affecting it.

The darkness pushed back at me. It wanted me to stop. People called out around me, but their words were lost in the wind.

All I knew was that I couldn't stop now.

If I stopped now, all would be lost.

I reached deep into my soul, digging until I found the root of my magic—the core where it began. It was like I was holding it in the palms of my hands.

Laila, my love, I'll see you soon, I thought.

Then I thrust every bit of my magic into the darkness, screaming as the last of it ripped out of my body and exploded into a bright, blinding light.

40

ANNIKA

THE LIGHT around Geneva consumed the Hell Gate.

It was sucked into the open chasm, eventually dimming and going out as the last bit of it disappeared inside. The opening closed back up, stitching back together until it healed completely.

All that remained was Geneva, sprawled in a heap of dust with her eyes closed. She looked more at peace than ever before.

The sky was bright and blue, the air still. No one said a word. They just stared at the land that had once been the Hell Gate in shock. If it hadn't been for the ruined buildings and bloodied corpses littering the ground, no one would have known that a supernatural battle had just occurred.

We didn't have a total number of casualties, but I had a sinking feeling that it was a lot.

Jacen took my hand, and I looked gratefully at him, his touch giving me strength. We would get through this —together. After all, I was the Earth angel. I still wasn't completely sure what that meant, but I had a feeling I was supposed to take the lead.

"She's gone, isn't she?" I asked Mary. "Geneva sacrificed herself to close the Hell Gate."

Mary pulled the sapphire ring out from under her shirt. The once gleaming gem was now dull—it had lost its sparkle completely.

"Geneva performed her Final Spell to save us all." She approached Geneva's corpse and clasped the ring inside one of Geneva's hands, bowing her head respectfully. "She —along with all the others who sacrificed their lives here today—will be given the heroic funeral they deserve."

Suddenly, two forms ran out of an alley and into the square—Princess Karina and a shifter in wolf form. The princess wielded a sword, her eyes wide in terror. The wolf's lips were pulled back, ready to fight.

My first thought was that the wolf was trying to attack her. The wolves that had witnessed the closing of the Hell Gate had stopped fighting, but what about the others who had been on the outskirt? However, it quickly became clear that they were running alongside each other—*with* each other.

Karina spun around, staring down the alley with her sword readied. "A monster is chasing us from the palace," she said through labored breaths. "No matter what we do, nothing kills her. She's unstoppable."

The wolf by her side shifted into an attractive man. Of course, in my mind he couldn't hold a candle to Jacen —no one could—but it was impossible not to appreciate his rugged good looks. "There's no use fighting her," he said, his strong voice echoing across the square. "We'll do our best to keep holding her off so you can get to safety. But if you want to live, you need to run."

Many wolves listened to his command—I assumed he had power in the pack, even before this moment.

I stood strong with Karina and her wolf, a sinking feeling in my stomach telling me that despite the Hell Gate being closed, this war was far from over. Jacen stood with me, along with Mary, Camelia, and a fair amount of vampires and wolves that appeared to be trained fighters. Rosella remained as well, although she stood behind us.

I doubted the blind vampire was a strong fighter, but since she was a psychic, I assumed that her remaining here was a good sign for the rest of us.

Soon, the monster that Karina and the wolf had

spoken of tore out of the alley—a petite woman with red eyes glinting in the sunlight. She flashed her razor sharp teeth and sank them into the neck of the wolf closest to her.

Screams erupted through the square, and many ran to attack at once. But it was no use.

I raised my heavenly sword and made my way through the chaos. "Stand down!" I commanded, pushing through the crowd to get closer to the demon.

Weapons stuck out from all parts of the demon's body, but she pulled them out and threw them toward the onlookers, moving so quickly that she was nearly a blur. Her targets fell to the ground, and she continued using her teeth to attack those closest to her.

I avoided being hit by a few knives that came my way, and then I jumped up and brought my sword down on the demon, slicing straight through her neck.

Her head rolled off her body, and both parts disintegrated into piles of ashes. Just like with Samael, all that remained in the ashes were her teeth.

I knelt down and picked up a single tooth, placing it into the same pocket that held Samael's.

Karina stepped up to my side and held out a hand. I took it, allowing her to help me up.

"You may not be an actual princess," she said. "But after that, you're royal in my book."

"Thanks," I said, and while I didn't voice it aloud, that meant a lot from her.

"What was that horrible creature?" She glanced down at the ashes, giving a slight shiver. "Noah and I tried everything to kill it, but nothing worked…"

I glanced at the man she'd emerged with, figuring that he was Noah—the infamous First Prophet of the wolves.

Despite Emmanuel telling me not to judge the wolves harshly, and despite Jacen believing that Noah was a "good guy," disgust filled me at the sight of him. Unlike Marigold, who'd been possessed and unable to stop Samael, Noah had allowed himself to be tricked by the demon. He'd gathered his people and led them to slaughter innocent vampires. *All* of the wolves had been gullible, but he most of all.

How could someone lead so many to a massacre without questioning what they were doing?

"That creature was a demon." Jacen stepped to my side, resting his hand on my arm and facing the crowd. "Annika was able to kill it because her sword was blessed by an angel."

41

ANNIKA

TOGETHER, Jacen and I told everyone the *truth* of what had happened.

The wolves were crushed that their Savior had never existed—and embarrassed that they'd believed Samael's lies so easily. But after seeing the Hell Gate erupt and the demon in the square, no one fought our words.

"The Hell Gate was closed, but the demon was still here," a wolf spoke up from the crowd. "Why?"

"Yeah," the vampire next to her chimed in. "Shouldn't the demon have disappeared with the Hell Gate?"

"I'm not sure," I said. "I *hope* that demon was left behind as some kind of fluke, but right now, I know as much as you."

"But you're an angel." Noah raised an eyebrow, his gaze challenging. "Shouldn't you know this stuff?"

I held his gaze and clenched my fists, trying to contain my frustration. Because he was right. As an angel and a leader, I *should* know this stuff. I hated that I couldn't give everyone the answers they deserved.

I wasn't sure what kind of leader I'd be—or if I'd be accepted as a leader at all—but I knew I didn't want to lie just to make people feel better.

"The demon was not a fluke." Rosella stepped forward, and silence descended upon the crowd. "It was the only demon remaining in the Vale, but hundreds of demons escaped the Hell Gate while it was open. With the Hell Gate sealed, no more can escape, but those who got out still roam the Earth."

A million questions came from the crowd at once. People were scared, and after seeing the demon that had bombarded the square, I couldn't blame them.

How were we supposed to beat *hundreds* of demons? What were the demons going to do now that they were on Earth?

How many more innocents would die because I'd failed to kill Samael when I'd first had the chance?

"Quiet!" Rosella raised her arms in the air, and once more, everyone obeyed her command. For someone so small, it was incredible how loud she could be. "I have the answers you seek. The situation is dire, yes, but it's not unbeatable. The demons have dispersed themselves throughout Earth, and they're determined to make Earth their home. They want to rid Earth of all supernaturals and rule with humans as their slaves. But demons are ancient creatures—older than most every other species' except the angels and gods. Time holds a different meaning to creatures so old, and the supernatural community outnumbers the demons, so they won't rush into anything. This gives us time to gather our strength and plan how we're going to defeat them. As you learned earlier, I was a psychic who was turned into a vampire, so my abilities are heightened. I can tell you with certainty—there are many possible outcomes to our war with the demons, and not all of them are grim. The world will be a darker place while demons roam freely, but we have a fair chance to defeat them and restore peace to Earth. We'll have to work together, but it *can* be done."

Hope filled me with Rosella's words. I trusted the psychic—if she foresaw victory as a possible future, then it must be true.

Mary stepped up next to Rosella and looked confidently out at the crowd. The two of them were a beacon of peace in their matching white Haven outfits. Somehow, amidst all the chaos, they'd avoided getting any stains on their clothing.

"The supernatural community is strongest when the

kingdoms are at peace and working together," Mary said, her eyes strong and calm. "I'd like to remind you that the Haven is open for all supernaturals who wish to live there, whether vampire, shifter, or witch. We always keep our own safe. We also protect peace amongst the supernatural community. The demons who have been released from the Hell Gate threaten that peace, and therefore I swear that the Haven will do everything possible to see every last demon returned to Hell where they belong."

People clapped at her words, speaking up in agreement and looking up at Mary as if she were a Savior herself.

I wanted to say that I too wanted to join the Haven, but I didn't. Something—I wasn't sure what exactly—held me back.

"We'll need to search the Vale for survivors and contact Prince Alexander to let him know it's safe to return," Jacen said, and then he turned to Karina and Noah. "You two came from the palace. Is there any word on Prince Scott and Princess Stephenie?"

"They didn't make it." From the horror in Karina's eyes, I had a feeling that there was more to the story than she'd said. However, now wasn't the time to probe for details.

"Very well." Jacen nodded, and then returned his

focus to Mary. "Can you send a witch envoy from the Haven to locate and retrieve Prince Alexander?"

"I'll send as many witches as we can spare to come to the aid of the Vale," Mary said. "We'll help in any way we can."

"Thank you," Jacen said. "I'll forever be in your debt for your help today."

"All I ask is that you do everything you can to retain the peace between kingdoms—especially in the trying times to come," Mary said. "But we have no time to waste before searching for survivors. Is this palace still intact?"

"It is," Noah said.

"Good," she said. "Bring all the survivors there, whether vampire, shifter, or human. Once we have an idea of how many made it through this war, we can figure out our next steps."

Everyone in the square dispersed, until Jacen, Mary, Camelia, Rosella, and I were left alone. The only other bodies that remained were those of the corpses. I did everything to keep from looking at them, but it was impossible not to see them—the reminders of my failure.

"Where will the two of you choose to go?" Mary asked Jacen and me. "Will you stay in the Vale to help rebuild, or join me in the Haven?"

Jacen looked to me, and I pressed my lips together, unsure how to answer.

I *wanted* to say I would help rebuild the Vale. But my angel instinct swelled inside of me, giving me the feeling that the Vale wasn't where I needed to be. However, the Haven wasn't where I needed to be, either.

"Annika doesn't belong in the Vale *or* the Haven." Rosella stepped forward with a folded piece of paper in her hands. "She belongs in Avalon."

42

ANNIKA

ROSELLA HANDED the paper to me, and I unfolded it, astounded at the beautiful drawing inside. It was a luscious, mountainous island in a horseshoe shape around a sparkling blue lake.

I wasn't sure if true paradise existed, but if it did, that island would be it.

"Where did you find this?" I asked. "Where is this place?"

"I've seen images in my mind of this island for my entire life," she said. "Only recently has it become clear enough for me to put to paper."

"You drew it?" I couldn't help but sound doubtful—how could she draw given that she was blind?

"I did," she said.

"How?"

"After sending you on your quest for the Grail, the image of the island became exceptionally clear in my mind," she said. "My hand took over, and I was finally able to bring it to life. Because this place—Avalon—is where you belong."

"Why?" I asked. "What waits for me at Avalon?"

"That's for you to find out," Rosella said. "I'm merely the messenger. But since you managed to get from the Tree of Life to the Vale, I'm sure you can figure out how to get from the Vale to Avalon."

Of course—I needed to teleport. To teleport, I needed to picture the place where I was going. This beautiful drawing gave me the ability to do just that.

"We'll go at once," I said, looking to Jacen. "Are you ready?"

"Whenever you are." He took my hands in his and gave them a small squeeze.

"Wait," Rosella said. "There's one more thing I need to tell you."

"What?" I bounced on my toes, as anxious as ever to go to Avalon and discover what awaited me there.

"You should take Camelia as well."

I glanced at the witch, disgust rolling through my body at the sight of her.

Camelia had sent Mike to his death. She'd hunted me down when I'd tried to escape the Vale. She'd locked me in a dungeon. She'd revealed my true identity to the vampires and had ordered me dead.

Now I was supposed to bring her with me to Avalon?

"Absolutely not," I said.

"For once, I agree with Annika." Camelia stuck her nose in the air, still as haughty as ever. "I'll be returning to the Haven."

"What if I were to tell you that Avalon is the only place where your child will be untraceable?" Rosella asked.

"Truly untraceable?" Camelia wrapped her arms around her stomach, her eyes fierce with a protectiveness I'd never seen in her before. "Even from the fae?"

"Even from the fae." Rosella nodded.

"Then I'll do anything to go to Avalon." Camelia turned to face me, desperation in her eyes. "You have every reason to hate me. But bringing me with you won't be for me. It'll be for my unborn child."

From there, she told me everything about the deal she'd made with Prince Devyn. She was desperate as she spoke. It was clear she would do anything to protect her child, even if that meant begging for my help.

"The fae can still get to my child at the Haven," she finished. "But since the fae can't trace us at Avalon, you *have* to bring us with you. Please."

I didn't like being told that I *had* to do anything. But

at the same time, Camelia had a point. Rosella wouldn't have made it up about Avalon being the only place untraceable by the fae. She also wouldn't have recommended that I bring Camelia with me for no reason.

Which meant I needed to consider bringing the witch to Avalon.

"I understand that you don't want to give up your child," I started, and Camelia nodded, her eyes bright and hopeful. "But you made a deal with Prince Devyn, and he's the child's father. Shouldn't he have a right to the child, too?"

"The fae are cold, manipulative creatures," Camelia said, which struck me as ironic, since it sounded like she was describing herself. "We know nothing of the Otherworld. I can't let my child be taken there. Please, let us come to Avalon. I'll do anything for you if you let us come with you. I swear it."

I turned to Rosella, still unconvinced by Camelia's begging. "Do you have any idea what will happen to Camelia's child if he or she goes to the Otherworld?" I asked.

"Not much," Rosella said. "My abilities only allow me to see what will happen on Earth—not on the other realms."

"I know a bit about the fae," Mary spoke up, and all eyes went to her. "I don't know much, but I know that they consider themselves to be a superior race—far superior than any other supernatural creature in the universe. They want to keep their race pure, which is why they keep to themselves in the Otherworld and only venture out if they receive something of value in return. I can't say for sure, because no one from Earth has ever gone to the Otherworld and returned to tell the tale, but I don't imagine they'll be welcoming to a child who is half-fae and half-witch."

Listening to Mary brought a hollow feeling to my stomach. If she was correct, that meant that once being brought to the Otherworld, Camelia's child would be condemned simply for the circumstance of his or her birth.

Camelia deserved to suffer the consequences of everything she'd done, but her child shouldn't have to pay for her mistakes, too.

"I don't trust you," I told Camelia. "After everything you've done to me, I'll never be able to trust you. But I trust Rosella, and I don't wish any harm upon your child, so I'll bring you to Avalon."

"Thank you." Camelia smiled—it was the first real smile I'd ever seen from her.

Jacen looked at Camelia like he was ready to rip her up in a second. "Try anything against us while there, and you *will* suffer the consequences," he warned. "I'll see to it myself."

"I won't try anything against either of you," she said. "I swear it. All I care about is that my child and I can stay safe in Avalon."

"I can bring you there, but I don't know if you staying there will be my decision to make," I said. "We have no idea what awaits us once we arrive."

"We don't," Jacen agreed. "But I'm ready to find out."

"Me too," I agreed, turning once more to Mary and Rosella. "I'm more thankful than you'll ever know for your support and guidance." I pulled my sword out of its sheath and handed it to Mary. "As a token of my thanks, I'd like you to have this."

"Are you sure?" Mary hesitated. "That sword was blessed by the angels themselves and given specifically to you."

"It was given to me so I could kill Samael," I said. "Now he's dead, and this sword is the only weapon on Earth that can kill demons. We'll figure out how to get more heavenly weapons soon—we'll *have* to, if we want to defeat the demons. But for now, the sword belongs where it can be put to good use. That's not at Avalon— that's with you."

"Thank you." Mary bowed her head in respect and took the sword from me. "I'll keep watch over it while you're at Avalon, but the sword will always be yours. You can ask for it back at any time with no questions asked. And if you ever need me, you'll always be welcome to visit the Haven."

"Don't worry—you haven't seen the last of me yet," I said. "But I do have one more question before I go."

"Yes?" she asked.

"The two humans—Raven and Susan," I started, referring to the humans Geneva had kidnapped and locked in a supernatural prison so she could use their DNA for the transformation potions we were using to disguise ourselves in the palace. "They were returned to their homes safely, right? The last I saw of them, they were passed out on your bed after being given a sleeping potion. I trust that you returned them, but I realized I haven't checked yet, so I just wanted to be sure."

"They were returned after you left for Norway, and are now safe at their homes in California," Mary said. "Geneva's memory potion worked perfectly. The humans won't remember a thing."

"It's for the best," I said. Susan had been traumatized by the ordeal, and Raven... well, who knew what the fiery redheaded human would have done if she hadn't had her memories of the supernatural world erased and replaced? Judging by how she'd tried to attack me and Mary at Mary's cabin—despite Mary and I *clearly* overpowering her—I had a feeling she was the type to jump headfirst into trouble without always stopping to think about the consequences.

She kind of reminded me of myself in that way.

"Yes, it certainly is for the best," Rosella agreed with a smile—a knowing sort of smile, like she was aware something she wasn't saying.

A part of me wanted to ask what the look was about. But if there was one thing I'd learned about the psychic, it was that she always spoke up when it was needed.

Whatever she knew would be revealed in time.

We said our goodbyes, although I made sure it was clear that they were "see you laters," and not goodbyes.

Then I took Camelia's hand—I was now holding onto both her and Jacen—pictured the image of Avalon that Rosella had drawn, and transported us there.

43

ANNIKA

WE ARRIVED ON A BEACH.

The second I felt the sand under my feet, I had a distinct feeling that I'd arrived *home*. The air was hot and humid, and I opened my eyes, expecting to see the tropical paradise from Rosella's drawing.

Instead, I saw an island filled with dead trees and ruined buildings. Everything was brown and gray. The sky was overcast, the sun barely shining through the thick clouds. I didn't even hear the chirping of birds or buzzing of insects.

It was like no one had been there for hundreds of years.

A long path nearby was the only thing somewhat intact, leading up to what appeared to have once been a castle on top of a mountain. But like everything else on the island, the castle was in shambles.

My heart ached for the island. What had happened to leave it such a mess?

Jacen also gazed around, looking as disheartened as I felt.

"Well." Camelia scrunched her nose as she looked around the ruins. "This can't be the right place."

"If you don't like it, you're free to leave." I kicked a nearby rock into the ocean, watching it disappear into the waves. Even the water was dark and murky—as if it had been polluted.

"Maybe you need time to rest," Jacen said to me. "We've been through a lot today. Once we've rested, you can try again to teleport us to Avalon."

"This *is* Avalon." Despite it looking nothing like the drawing, I knew in my bones that this was the same place.

"Okay." Jacen didn't doubt me—I loved that he trusted me, just the same as I trusted him. "Maybe there's a spell on the island? An illusion spell or something that isn't letting us see it for what it is—like the spell on that cabin in Norway."

"It would take an extraordinary amount of magic to perform a spell like that—I don't even think Geneva could have done such a thing," Camelia said. "Not that it matters, because there's definitely no spell on this island."

"How can you be sure?" I asked.

"Because there's no magic on this island at all."

"But Rosella said we'd be untraceable here," I said. "I assumed that meant there was some kind of magical barrier around the island…"

"There's nothing," she said. "The island's a total dead zone."

I nodded, since I felt it too. The island was hollow and empty. I'd wanted to find paradise at Avalon, but it was uninhabitable. Of course we could explore and see if we found anything, but from where we were standing, finding any life looked hopeless.

Suddenly, I saw something in the corner of my eye.

I whipped my head around to see what it was, finding smoke rising from a crumbling chimney in the ruined castle.

"There." I pointed to the smoke. "Someone's in the castle."

I tried to teleport us there, but it didn't work. It likely had something to do with the island being a "magical dead zone."

Instead, I hurried to the start of the path. Jacen and Camelia followed quickly on my heels.

"We're just going toward the castle even though we

have no idea what's waiting inside?" Camelia's eyes widened.

If I didn't know better, I might have thought she was scared.

"It's a good thing I still have my daggers." Jacen handed one of them to me, holding onto the other for himself.

We both walked ahead of Camelia, and I internally questioned my decision to give my sword to Mary so easily. It had felt right at the time, but if a demon waited in that castle, we wouldn't be able to kill it.

I shook away the fear and walked faster up the mountain.

The castle was massive—it was closer in size to an academy than a home. The stones were browned and crumbling, but of course they didn't have any vines crawling on them, since there was no greenery to be found on the island.

The path led up to a clearing in front of the castle. Jacen and I led the way across, eventually reaching the giant arched doors. One of the doors was slightly ajar, as if the castle were waiting for our arrival. The wood was so eaten away that I feared it would collapse from a single touch.

I held my breath as I pushed on it, glad when it stayed intact as it creaked open.

Inside was a tall foyer filled with dusty old furniture. The furniture looked like it was once brightly colored, but it was impossible to truly tell under the layers of filth. The walls were cracked and crumbling, and a chandelier full of cobwebs had fallen to the floor.

I led the way down a hall to the right, since that was where the smoke had been coming from.

Suddenly, Jacen stopped. He pointed forward, motioning to his ear.

People were talking in a room nearby. I couldn't tell how many people there were, and I couldn't make out what they were saying, but the voices sounded distinctly female.

I nodded at Jacen, and we followed the sound of the voices. Camelia stayed behind us, rubbing her arms as she walked. I couldn't blame her—the castle *was* rather drafty.

We stopped in front of the wooden door where the voices were coming from.

I glanced at Jacen and Camelia, but they both looked to me. I got the message—I was the one Rosella sent here, so whatever we did next was my call.

I took a deep breath, preparing to open the door. But before I could, someone spoke to us from inside.

"What are you waiting for?" the voice said. "Come in

and join us. We've only been waiting on this dreary, boring island for days."

I pushed the door open and came face to face with the three mages from Norway.

ANNIKA

DAHLIA, Violet, and Iris sat around a huge round table in front of a burning fireplace. Unlike the rest of the furniture in the castle, the table gleamed like new, as if the mages had spent time cleaning it in preparation for our arrival.

In the center of the table was the Holy Grail.

"Welcome to Avalon." Violet stood up and smiled, fluffing the skirt of her elaborate purple gown. "I'm glad to see that you survived your journey."

"Thanks to you," I said. "We wouldn't have made it to the Tree of Life without your help."

"We know." Dahlia's lips turned up in a flirty smile, her eyes focused on Jacen. "Helping you was our pleasure."

Jacen stepped closer to me, and I stood straighter, relieved he was making it clear that he was taken.

"I take it that you all know each other?" Camelia asked, looking from me to the mages and back again.

"This is Dahlia, Violet, and Iris." I pointed to each of them as I said their names. "They're mages—they helped me and Jacen get to the Tree of Life."

"Mages don't exist." Camelia crossed her arms and looked suspiciously at the three sisters. "They're from storybooks—they aren't *real*."

"We heard that witches didn't like to acknowledge our existence." Iris twisted a strand of hair around her finger, looking amused. "However, it's true. Humans and mages mated to create witches, which is how your kind came to be."

"I don't believe you." Camelia curled her upper lip in distaste. "Prove it."

"We don't have time for that right now," Dahlia chided. "We're here on important business regarding Annika—not for you. If you have a problem with that, we'll have no choice but to remove you from the island." She snapped her fingers, and a nearby couch vanished— as if it had never been there in the first place.

Camelia's face paled, and her hands rushed to her stomach. "I have no problem with that," she said, sounding meeker than ever.

"I thought not," Dahlia said, and with that, all three sisters turned their attention back to me.

"Come, join us at the table." Violet motioned to the throne-like seats. There were thirteen of them in all, including the ones the mages currently occupied. "We'd offer tea, but as I'm sure you've seen, Avalon is lacking such basic necessities at the moment."

I pulled out a chair to join them, and Jacen and Camelia followed my lead. I nodded respectfully at Camelia, glad that for once, the witch was keeping her mouth shut.

Once seated, the group of us only filled up half of the table. It was an awkward way to have a conversation, but the table and chairs were the only functional pieces of furniture in the castle, so we'd have to make do.

"I'd like to start by saying congratulations," Dahlia said with a smile.

"Thank you." I shrugged, looking down at the table. "But I'm not sure I deserve it."

"Why do you say that?"

"Because I failed." I looked back up at her, my heart dropping as I said the words out loud. "I was supposed to stop Samael from opening the Hell Gate, but I couldn't do it. The Hell Gate opened, and now all those demons are loose..." I paused, shivering at the thought of the red-eyed creatures wandering the Earth who were determined to kill all the supernaturals and take the humans as their slaves.

"You didn't fail," Violet said. "The Hell Gate was always supposed to open. If it hadn't opened now, it would have opened at some point in the future. In fact, if it hadn't opened now—if you'd killed Samael while he was possessing Marigold—*then* you would have failed."

"What do you mean?" I tilted my head in confusion. "If I'd killed Samael while he'd been possessing Marigold, I would have stopped him from opening the Hell Gate."

"Then you would have killed an innocent and not been worthy to be the leader of Avalon," she said simply.

"And the Hell Gate *still* would have opened at some point in the future," Iris added. "It would have been opened in a different way, and likely in a different place, but it still would have happened."

"Hold up." Jacen placed his hands on the table, and everyone looked to him. "Are you saying that this was some sort of test to see if Annika was a worthy leader of Avalon?"

"That's precisely what we're saying." Dahlia's eyes gleamed in approval—she looked at Jacen like he was her favorite student who'd just answered a question correctly in class. Then she turned to me, and continued, "You showed that you possessed the strength, determination, and the ability to make quick decisions in the heat of battle by finding the Grail. But after being turned into an Earth angel, you needed to prove that you had the empathy, mercy, and kindness required of the future leader of Avalon. A leader without those qualities turns into a tyrant, and after what happened to the previous generations of Nephilim, we couldn't have that."

I nodded, remembering what Mary had told me of the Nephilim of the past. Their prejudice against other supernaturals started the Great War, which they'd lost.

"So Emmanuel never wanted me to kill Samael while he possessed Marigold," I realized.

"Yes," Dahlia said. "Marigold was an innocent being used in a terrible way. You demonstrated empathy by being unable to kill her, despite the horrible things Samael was doing while possessing her body. Most others wouldn't have done the same."

"But she died anyway." Tears filled my eyes at the memory of her slitting her own throat while Samael possessed her body.

"Samael was always going to either die in that body or kill it to perform the blood spell to open the Hell Gate," Iris said. "There was nothing you could have done to save Marigold. I'm sorry."

I swallowed down the tears, since it made sense. But

it still didn't make me feel better about the young witch's death.

"Empathy toward Marigold was only one part of the test," Dahlia said. "You were also tested on two other qualities—mercy and kindness."

"Was kindness Camelia?" I asked, glancing at the witch. "Bringing her to Avalon despite all the awful things she's done?"

"No." Dahlia smiled. "The choice to allow Camelia to come to Avalon or not was a test of mercy. Camelia's problem is not your own, and you had every right not to help her after all she did to you and to those you love. Yet, you showed her mercy. There aren't many who would have done the same."

"I almost didn't," I muttered. "She's only here because of her child."

"Nonetheless, you did," Dahlia said. "Showing her mercy was an act of kindness, but your test of kindness was something else. Do you remember the wolf shifter you encountered in the alley?"

"Of course," I said, since that had only happened a few hours ago.

"She was your enemy," Dahlia continued. "She was trying to kill you. But you made a blood oath with her and let her live."

"Anyone would have done that," I said.

"No." She held her gaze with mine. "They wouldn't have."

I took a few seconds to absorb her words, unsure what to say. "How do you know all of this, anyway?" I asked. "You weren't at the Vale during the battle."

"We have our ways." Iris smiled knowingly.

"We also have this." Violet reached down into a bag by her feet, pulling out a piece of parchment with writing on it and a golden pen. The pen had one of those fancy tips meant for calligraphers.

She placed both items down on the table and looked at me expectantly.

"What's that?" I asked.

"A contract," Dahlia said. "For you to become the official leader of Avalon."

45

ANNIKA

"AFTER YOU DRANK from the Grail, Emmanuel sent us this contract to give to you if you passed all three tests," Dahlia continued. "All you have to do is read it and sign."

She handed the contract to me and placed the pen on the table in front of me.

"Oh, and the pen has no ink of its own," she added. "You'll have to use your own blood."

I ran a finger over the golden pen. A few months ago, using my blood as ink would have disgusted me, but now I wasn't surprised at all. Supernaturals *loved* binding contracts and making promises with blood. Anyway, I healed quickly now, so it was no big deal.

I lifted the contract and read through it.

Once finished, I lowered it and looked back up, finding everyone watching me expectantly.

"Well?" Violet asked, glancing toward the pen.

"Can Jacen and I step outside to talk?" My voice shook as I spoke. "Alone?"

"Take all the time you need." Dahlia rolled her eyes—she was clearly anxious for me to sign the contract. "The door on the other side of the room leads out to the garden."

I hadn't noticed the door before. It was small and wooden, but thankfully still intact.

I stood up—taking the contract with me—and walked toward the door, glad when Jacen followed by my side. He pushed it open and held it out for me to walk through.

"Thanks," I said once we'd stepped outside.

The garden was in a courtyard, and like everything else in Avalon, it was brown and dead. I wouldn't have even *known* it was supposed to be a garden if Dahlia hadn't referred to it as such beforehand.

"You know they can probably still listen in on us," he said, glancing at the shut door. "Right?"

"I know." I took a deep breath, feeling like I could finally breathe again now that we weren't inside the musty, run-down castle. "I just needed some fresh air."

"Because of what you read in the contract?"

"Yeah." I sat down on a wrought-iron bench, glad when Jacen joined me.

That was when I remembered that even though it was cloudy out, it was still daytime.

"Is the sun bothering you?" I asked. "If it is, we can go back inside." I started to stand up, but he reached for my hand, stopping me.

"It's so cloudy that I can barely feel the sun at all," he said, glancing up at the gray sky.

"This island *is* pretty depressing," I agreed.

He put his arm around me, and I snuggled into him, reminded of when we'd sat like this in the boat as we'd watched the Northern Lights. Now that it was just the two of us, I felt so much more relaxed than when I'd been in there with the mages and Camelia hovering over my every word.

"Signing the contract will make me the official ruler of Avalon," I said.

"This place is falling apart." He looked around at the dead garden and the crumbling walls of the castle, his nose crinkling in distaste. "You're going to make an incredible leader, but you deserve a kingdom better than *this*."

"It says that after I sign, the island will be blessed by the angels," I said. "Their blessing will apparently make Avalon the safest place on Earth. And once I sign the contract—*if* I sign the contract—I'm supposed to use the Holy Grail to create an army of Nephilim to defeat the demons on Earth." I said the last part all in one breath, the weight of the responsibility still yet to sink in.

"And you'll be the leader of that army." Adoration shined in his eyes. "As the only angel to walk upon the Earth, you'll be the perfect leader for it."

"I'm an *Earth* angel," I corrected him. "Not a born angel. It's different."

"You're an angel," he repeated. "The first one to walk on the Earth for thousands of years. It's incredible."

"Thanks." My cheeks heated—I still didn't feel like I deserved to be an actual angel. I doubted it would ever feel real. "But back to the contract—it says I can use the Holy Grail to turn humans into Nephilim, similar to the way that Emmanuel turned me into an Earth angel. I just have to pour some of my blood into the Grail, and they'll drink it. If they're strong enough, their blood will turn into the blood of a dormant Nephilim —like I was before I killed Laila and activated my powers."

"And if they're not strong enough?" he asked.

"They'll die."

He nodded, his eyes intense. "Then we'll make sure they're strong," he said. "We'll train them until they're ready to drink from the Grail."

"Their lives will be in my hands," I said. "I'm not sure it's a responsibility I want to have. And even after drinking from the Grail, their powers won't be activated. They have to make a supernatural kill first."

"That kill can be a demon?" he asked.

"It can be a regular demon—not a greater demon," I repeated what I'd read in the contract. "Only a full Nephilim can kill a greater demon."

"Okay." He paused, glancing out into the dead garden before returning his attention to me. "So we'll have them kill regular demons. There are also plenty of rogue supernaturals—ones who aren't a part of any of the kingdoms—who harm humans."

"So you want to find those rogues and have the Nephilim kill them to ignite their powers?"

"It's an option," he said. "And the kingdoms will need our help, too—they won't want the demons on the Earth any more than we do. They might even *give* us any dangerous rogues they find so one of our dormant Nephilim can kill it to activate their powers. It would help us build our army."

Our army. A ball of anxiety formed in my throat at the words.

"You're assuming the supernaturals would welcome a new generation of Nephilim," I said. "But what if they don't? They fought a war to get *rid* of the Nephilim. Why would they want the Nephilim to return?"

"Because like you said, only Nephilim can kill greater

demons," he answered quickly. "Out of the hundreds of demons that escaped, I don't know how many are greater demons, but we're more likely to beat them if you don't have to fight each one alone. We need more Nephilim."

"We do," I agreed, although I doubted the supernaturals would accept the return of the Nephilim so easily. "But where are we going to find humans who want to do this?" I pulled my legs up and wrapped my arms around them, trying to make sense of all the questions racing through my mind. "I won't take them by force."

"You won't have to," he said. "There are billions of humans in the world. Surely we'll be able to find some who want to join us. And don't forget—we'll have the support of the Haven, and likely the other supernatural kingdoms as well. I'd place my bet on Alexander and the Vale helping us. They all want the demons gone as badly as we do."

I glanced at the contract, still doubtful. "I'm just not sure I'm ready for this," I admitted. "I only recently came into my powers myself. How am I supposed to lead an *army?*"

"The angels wouldn't have chosen you if they didn't think you could succeed," he said.

"Or maybe I was the only choice they had, so taking a chance on me was better than nothing."

"This is your decision." Jacen sat straighter, determination shining in his gaze. "After everything we've been through, I know you can do it. And you won't have to do it alone. If you accept, I'll be by your side helping you every step of the way. It's going to be a lot of hard work, but we can do it. Together. You won't be able to get rid of me even if you tried."

"That's a pretty big statement to make." I smiled for the first time since we'd come out to the garden. "Especially given that we're both immortal now."

"It's an easy statement to make," he said. "Because I love you, Annika."

He said it so easily, as if loving me were as natural as breathing.

The words took my breath away. They also made me realize what I'd known from the first time I'd laid eyes on him at the Christmas Eve festival in the village—before I knew he was a vampire prince, back when I thought he was another human blood slave of the Vale.

"I've loved you since the moment I saw you." It was easy for me to say, because it was true. "Why else would I have been crazy enough to sneak you into the Tavern's attic when those vampire guards were after you?"

"It *was* pretty reckless," he agreed.

"I guess people do crazy, reckless things when they're

in love." My cheeks heated at the word, although now that it was finally said, I felt closer to Jacen than ever.

"Crazy things like trying to sneak a wanted blood slave that I'd just met out of the Vale to save her life?" He raised an eyebrow in challenge.

"Yes." I laughed. "Just like that."

He leaned forward and kissed me, neither of us needing to say any more. We loved each other. And he was right—we *could* do this. As long as I had Jacen by my side, I felt like I could do anything I set my mind to.

Recruiting humans to turn into an army of Nephilim to eventually defeat the demons that had been unleashed upon the Earth was an incredibly daunting task, but I couldn't live with myself if I didn't try.

"Thank you," I said, once the kiss was eventually broken.

"For what?" he asked.

"For believing in me, and more importantly, for helping me learn to believe in myself."

With that, I reached for the contract and the pen.

46

ANNIKA

ENERGY RACED through my veins as I stared down at the contract.

Once I went through with this, nothing would ever be the same.

"You're sure about this?" Jacen asked. "If you sign, it needs to be because it's what *you* want, and not because it's what others expect of you."

"A moment ago you were trying to convince me I could do this, and now you're having second thoughts?" I tilted my head playfully, smiling up at him.

"No seconds thoughts here," he said. "You're going to make an incredible queen of Avalon."

"Not a queen," I said. "I don't know what I'll call myself, but after the Vale I've had enough of royalty for the rest of my life."

"Understandable," he said.

Then I held out my wrist and looked at him expectantly. "I need to use my blood as ink," I reminded him. "I was hoping you would do the honors?"

"It would be my pleasure."

He lowered his mouth to my wrist, kissing it gently before his fangs punctured my skin.

Golden blood released, and ecstasy rolled through my body as his venom entered my system. But he barely took a sip before pulling away.

His eyes were dark and dilated—he clearly wanted more—and my cheeks heated under his tantalizing gaze.

"Focus, Annika." His voice was silky smooth, like music to my ears. "Or you'll heal before you can sign the contract."

He was right—despite how distracting he was, I needed to hurry. So I pressed on my wound to release more blood. It was so strange to bleed gold instead of red—yet one more thing in my life that I doubted I would get used to.

I dipped the pen in the blood and signed *Annika Pearce* on the bottom line of the parchment.

Once I lifted the pen from the paper, the ink started to glow. The glow spread out—first along the parchment, and then further and further out into the garden.

As the golden glow rippled outward, the ground

turned from brown to green, and the trees and plants unraveled into vibrant, colorful flowers. They came alive like a time lapse of winter turning to spring. The stone fountain in the center—previously dry and cobwebbed—cleaned itself up and bubbled with flowing water. A butterfly landed on my finger, and I held my hand out in wonder, watching it spread its wings and fly through the garden.

The golden glow rippled out over the castle, and as it did, the castle reassembled itself until it was like new. Even the clouds had cleared from the sky, the sun shining brightly down upon us.

Jacen held out his hand, looking at it in amazement. "The sun," he said, his voice reflecting the wonder upon his face. "It doesn't burn."

"How's that possible?" I asked.

"I don't know," he said. "All I know is that for the first time since being turned into a vampire, the sun isn't hurting me."

I smiled and basked with him in the sunlight, taking a deep breath of the sweet garden air.

Now more than ever, I finally felt like I was home.

ANNIKA

WE MARVELED at the garden for a few more minutes before heading back inside.

Just like the outside of the castle, the inside was now warm and inviting, sparkling like new.

The mages and Camelia waited at the table where we'd left them.

"I take it you signed the contract?" Dahlia asked.

I walked to the table and placed the pen and signed contract next to the Holy Grail. "I did," I confirmed. "But what exactly happened when I signed it? Jacen can now walk in the sunlight without any pain... that shouldn't be possible for a vampire."

"The moment you signed the contract, Avalon was blessed by the angels and restored to its previous glory," Iris said with a smile. "The blessing of the angels offers the highest possible protection. Only those with angel blood or those who have been invited by those with angel blood will be able to find Avalon, and the island will provide for all those who reside here."

"So it's true, then," Camelia said. "The fae won't be able to track me or my child."

"It's true," Violet said. "And any vampire on Avalon will be able to walk in the sunlight without being burned. However, these protections only apply to those inside the island's protective shield."

"So I'll never be able to leave Avalon," Camelia realized. "Nor will my child."

"Correct," Violet said. "However, as long as Annika permits you to stay, you and your daughter will be safe from the fae."

"Daughter?" Camelia's eyes lit up. "I'm having a girl?"

"I'm afraid I've said too much." Violet pursed her lips and looked away, as if embarrassed for saying what she had.

Camelia turned to me, looking more vulnerable than ever. "You'll let me stay?" she asked. "Please?"

"As long as you remain loyal to me and Avalon," I said, since given the situation, I couldn't say no. But that didn't erase everything she'd done. "Your daughter has done nothing wrong, so she'll always have a home here. But if you make one wrong move against me—or against anyone on the island—I'll send you packing in a heartbeat. Understood?"

"Understood." Camelia lowered her eyes—her first move of deference toward me as a leader.

I nodded, knowing in my heart that this was the right decision. And while I doubted I would ever be able to forgive Camelia, I had a feeling that this pregnancy might change her for the better.

"Come with me." Dahlia stood from the table, lifting her gown as she walked toward the door that led to the hall. "It's time that you saw the *real* Avalon."

I took Jacen's hand, and together we walked through the magnificent castle. It was like something out of a fairy tale, and I couldn't wait to explore all the halls and rooms. But for now, we followed Dahlia toward the main entrance—the one we'd come in through earlier.

She threw the doors open, and I gasped at the beauty before me.

The island was now identical to the drawing Rosella had given me. It was green and luscious, full of hydrangeas in tons of vibrant colors. The clear blue lakes sparkled, and waterfalls roared with life as they pounded through the forested mountains before us.

"It's beautiful." Tears filled my eyes as I looked out at the island.

"Oh—there's one more thing you might want to

know," Dahlia said with a knowing smile. "You see all the lakes and waterfalls?"

"Yes," I said, since it was impossible to miss them.

"That's not regular water," she said. "It's heavenly water, blessed by the angels itself."

I gripped the handle of the dagger sheathed to my waist, power flowing through my veins as I stared out at the waterfalls and lakes. Because the water before us would do far more than provide sustenance to those who lived here.

It would give us a way to defeat the demons.

And I was going to build an army to do just that, here with Jacen in our new home—Avalon.

48

KARINA

WITH THE HELP of the wolves and vampires of the Vale, plus many citizens of the Haven, we were able to get basic clean up of the Vale done in a little over a week. There was still a lot more to be done—many of the buildings needed reconstructing after the explosion of the Hell Gate—but at least it was a start.

Alexander returned with his followers and assumed his position as king. One of the first things he did as king was declare equality for all those in the Vale. He was allowing wolves to live in the town, alongside vampires and humans. Not only that, but he gave the humans a choice to either stay in the Vale, return to their homes, or go to Avalon to see if they had what it took to become a Nephilim.

A surprising amount of them chose Avalon. Annika

would be coming in a few days to retrieve all the humans and supernaturals who wanted to learn to fight demons and bring them to the mysterious island where they'd start their training. Until then, they helped with the clean up.

The humans who chose to return home had their memories of the supernatural world wiped beforehand. Those who stayed were still required to donate blood in exchange for a place to live—after all, vampires still needed to eat—but they would no longer be denied the food and luxuries that were previously only available to vampires.

King Alexander truly meant it when he said that all who lived in the Vale were now equal.

Now, I stood in the mountains alongside all those who had fought in the war, watching the flames die out on the funeral pyre for the dead. Noah stood next to me, and we held hands the entire time.

Once the pyre ended, we headed back to the room in the palace where we were staying as we decided where we wanted to go from here.

I'd been thinking about my future a lot recently. And the longer I was at the Vale, the more I realized that I didn't belong here. While the war wasn't my fault—it was Samael and the demons' faults—I still held myself responsible for the role I'd played in the destruction of this once beautiful kingdom.

Even as I lay in Noah's arms once most of the kingdom was fast asleep, I couldn't shake the guilt of what I'd done.

"You're still awake?" Noah murmured in my ear.

"I can't sleep." I rotated to face him. "I keep thinking about where to go from here. I know Alexander told us that we're welcome to stay, but it doesn't feel right."

"I understand." His thumb traced patterns along my forearm, sending a pleasurable chill through my body. "I don't feel right staying in the Vale, either. Not after all the destruction I helped cause."

"That *we* helped cause," I reminded him. "I played a big role in it, too."

His eyes darkened, and he nodded, although he said nothing.

I had a feeling that the guilt he was holding onto was more than I—more than maybe *anyone* involved in the war—could possibly understand.

"Where do you want to go?" he asked.

"I've been thinking about it," I said. "And I want to go to the Haven."

"The Haven?" He sounded surprised. "Not Avalon?"

"Avalon is a training ground—humans and supernaturals alike will learn to be great fighters there," I said.

"But I already know how to fight. My experience will be best put to use at the Haven."

He said nothing for a few seconds, taking in my words. "Are you sure?" he finally asked.

"I'm sure." I swallowed, nervous to ask my next question. "You'll come with me… right?"

"If it makes you happy, then yes, I'll go to the Haven with you."

I smiled and snuggled into him, relief filling my veins at his response. He was coming with me. I wouldn't be alone.

I should be happy. But something felt off. I couldn't pinpoint what it was, but the answer pulled at the back of my mind, begging to be set free.

I just hoped everything would come together once we arrived at the Haven.

49

KARINA

THE NEXT MORNING, Mary sent the witch Shivani to bring us to the Haven. Shivani supplied us each with a change of clothes—the traditional, white garb worn by all Haven citizens. Once we'd changed, she held our hands and transported us there.

We appeared in the courtyard, and she escorted us into the main building, as it would take some time for our cabin to be prepared.

"You've arrived just in time for dinner," she said with a smile. "All citizens of the Haven are encouraged to dine together. Please, follow me."

We followed her down the brightly colored hall in silence.

Noah kept picking at his clothes, as if he couldn't get comfortable in them. It made no sense to me, since the uniform of the Haven was far more comfortable than the constrictive gowns I'd worn in the Carpathian Kingdom.

Eventually, Shivani opened the doors to a large dining hall, spacious enough to seat all the citizens of the Haven.

Like all the public spaces of the Haven, it was furnished in bright, warm colors. The food smelled delicious—like the flavorful exotic spices used to prepare Indian dishes. Vampires, witches, and shifters all shared tables with each other, chatting and laughing as they enjoyed their meals.

That was when I saw him.

He had dark hair and soulful eyes, and when our gazes met, everything else in the room blurred. He was all that remained clear, and looking at him pulled at that place in the back of my mind—at the something I should know but couldn't seem to remember.

"Karina," he breathed out my name and rushed toward me, his hands joining mine as he beamed down at me. His touch sent an electric jolt through my body, and his hands fit perfectly around mine, as if they'd held them many times before. "You found me."

"I'm sorry." I knew I should drop my hands from his —holding hands with a man I didn't know wasn't proper—but I couldn't bring myself to do it. "Have we met?"

"What are you talking about?" he asked. "It's me. Peter."

"Peter," I repeated his name, the syllables sounding *right* on my tongue.

This must be the same Peter that Noah had told me about—the one he claimed I was determined to bring back from the dead. But how could it be? This Peter was here—he was *alive*. From the story Noah had told me, the Peter I'd claimed to love had died in the Great War. He was lost to me forever.

Unless I'd managed to bring him back… by giving up my memories of him in return.

"You don't remember." His eyes dimmed, and my heart dropped at knowing I'd disappointed him.

"I'm sorry," I repeated. "Are you sure that you know me?"

"I more than know you," he said. "I love you. And you love me. At least, you did."

"Is there somewhere we can go to talk?" I asked, suddenly aware of the hundreds of eyes watching us in the dining room. "Alone?"

"Certainly." He straightened, ever the gentleman. "We can go to my cabin. Can your chaperone get settled here alone?" He glanced at Noah, and my heart sank once more.

Noah had stepped away from Peter and me, unable to meet my eyes. One glance at his face showed that he was crushed.

"That won't be necessary," Noah said, wiping all emotion from his expression. "I'm going to return to the Vale. Annika is coming in a few days to assess the volunteers who want to go to Avalon, and I want to be there for that."

"You want to go to Avalon?" His confession hurt me.

I thought he wanted to come here with me.

"I do." His eyes took on a fierceness that I hadn't seen in him since he believed he was the First Prophet of the wolves. "If it hadn't been for me, that Hell Gate wouldn't have opened. I need to do everything I can to banish those demons back to Hell where they belong. To do that, I have to train to be a better fighter. I have to go to Avalon."

"I understand," I said, since I did—his reasons were similar to why I'd wanted to come to the Haven. "But if you feel that way, why did you come here with me?"

"Because I thought you needed me," he said. "But now that you've reunited with Peter, I can see that you don't."

"That's not true…" I said, although my voice wavered as I spoke.

"It is." He leaned forward and placed a chaste kiss on my forehead. "You belong here—with him."

I wanted to tell him he was wrong, but I couldn't. "Will you at least keep in contact with me?" I asked instead. "So I know how you're doing?"

He stepped back, his eyes cold. "I think it's best that we go our separate ways for now," he said.

His words hurt, but I nodded, since I understood. Noah cared deeply for me, just as I had for him. As I *still* did for him.

But the moment I'd seen Peter, I knew that what I felt for Noah hadn't been love. I cared for Noah as a friend, I'd depended on him and trusted him during a difficult time, and he was undeniably attractive. But we weren't meant to be.

While I couldn't remember my time with Peter, my feelings for him and the way my body reacted to him were undeniable. I'd truly loved him. I *still* loved him. With him, my soul felt whole.

And so I followed Peter back to his cabin, ready to tell him what I knew, and ready to make new memories… together.

NOAH

LEAVING Karina with Peter was the hardest thing I'd ever done. But I saw the way she looked at him.

With him, she was finally home.

I loved Karina, but she would never return those feelings. And because I loved her, I wanted her to be happy. She would be happy with Peter. There was no place for me in her life anymore—at least, not the way I wanted there to be.

I truly *had* loved her enough to give up the idea of Avalon for the Haven. But that was no longer relevant. And so, Shivani returned me to the Vale, where as promised, Annika arrived a few days later to assess the volunteers and decide if she thought there would be a place for us in Avalon.

I stepped into the small room for my individual

assessment, coming face to face with the angel who had set all of this into motion.

I'd only seen her once before—right after the Hell Gate had been closed. She radiated strength and determination, although her gaze held a softness that made me feel at ease in her presence. Or maybe I felt at ease because she dressed simply, in jeans and a tank top. I wasn't sure what I'd expected an angel to wear, but it hadn't been that.

The only things that hinted she was a powerful leader were the sword strapped to her back and the dagger on her side.

"The First Prophet." She raised an eyebrow. "I wasn't expecting to see you here today."

"I'd like to come to Avalon to train." I held her gaze, not wanting to appear weak. "If you'll have me, of course."

She eyed me up in what felt like the longest few seconds of my life.

"The demon Samael slipped into your mind and planted visions in your dreams," she finally said. "You accepted his suggestions without question and gathered packs of wolves to kill innocent vampires."

Her accusation made me hang my head in shame. "I know what I've done," I said, forcing myself to meet her eyes again. "*Everyone* knows what I've done. Which is why I feel even more of a responsibility to help send every last demon back to Hell where they belong."

"Only Nephilim can kill greater demons," she said. "You're aware of this—correct?"

"I am," I said. "But with proper weapons, anyone can kill lesser demons. Supernaturals may not be able to transition into Nephilim, but we *can* help you fight. At least, that's what we were told when we learned you were accepting volunteers to come train at Avalon."

"It's true," she said. "However, it's important that our warriors are strong in both body *and* mind. You showed weakness by allowing Samael to get into your head and by believing him without question. Also, Avalon is not a place to go to hide from heartbreak."

"How do you know about that?" I asked.

"I've been in contact with Mary," she said. "She informed me about what happened at the Haven. I understand that you're hurt, but running away from problems has never helped solve them."

"I'm not running away," I said. "I wanted to go to Avalon from the start. I only went to the Haven for Karina."

Just saying her name sent daggers through my heart.

I swallowed to get rid of the pain, but I feared that the loss of what was only just starting to form between the princess and me would never go away.

"You'll heal in time," Annika said, as if she knew what I was thinking.

My emotions were probably written all over my face, so I straightened my shoulders, composing myself. "My personal life won't interfere with my training," I said. "I can't stay in the Vale. I'll never be able to look at the packs without being reminded how I failed them. Avalon is the only place where I can try to make this right—it's the only place where I'll have purpose again."

"I'm sorry, but I don't feel like you're a good fit for Avalon." She glanced at the door, her easy dismissal feeling like a punch to my gut. "Please send the next applicant in."

I turned and headed toward the door, but halfway there, I stopped in my tracks. I couldn't leave this room without doing everything possible to get to Avalon.

And so, I turned around, facing the Earth angel once more.

She tilted her head, as if surprised by my move.

"I'm a good fighter." I stood straighter, keeping my voice strong and confident. "You're right—I *should* have questioned the visions sent to me by Samael. I didn't, and because of that, hundreds were killed. I know more will die because of the demons that were released. I'll never forgive myself for that. All I can do is devote the rest of my life to sending them back to Hell. Training at

Avalon and fighting with the Nephilim is the best way I can do that. So tell me, Your Highness—"

"Annika," she interrupted me. "We still haven't developed a chain of command in Avalon, but it definitely won't have anything to do with royalty. So for now, please call me Annika."

"Annika." I nodded, although it felt strange to address an angel so casually. "Is there anything I can do to change your mind?"

She pressed her lips together, and I held my breath, bracing for her to dismiss me a second time.

"Yes," she said, and I blinked, stunned by her answer. "If you can bring me the teeth of ten demons that you've killed, I'll allow you to live and train in Avalon."

"That's it?" I waited for more, because surely there must be a catch.

"Do you want to bring me twenty teeth instead?" She tilted her head, a playful smile on her lips.

"No," I said, since the fewer teeth she required, the sooner I could get to Avalon. "Ten is good."

"I thought so." She reached for her dagger and pulled it out of its sheath, holding it out to me. "This dagger has been dipped in heavenly water, giving it the power to kill demons. Make sure not to lose it—I won't give you another one."

"Thank you." I took the dagger and gripped it tightly,

prepared to guard it with my life. "Where should I go to find the demons?"

"That's for you to figure out," she said. "In the meantime, I'm going to be busy training the new recruits, so only contact me once you have the ten demon teeth. If you come to me before then, my offer will be revoked."

"Understood," I said. "Thank you for this chance."

"You're welcome." She smiled—she was so warm and genuine that I knew she'd make an excellent leader. "Now, go send the next volunteer in."

I headed toward the door again, my mind racing with ideas of where to start demon hunting. I'd always wanted to see America—there were rumors about supernaturals secretly roaming free in America, unattached to any kingdom.

I could start in California and make my way east from there.

"And Noah?" Annika asked as I laid my hand on the doorknob.

I looked at her over my shoulder, waiting for her to continue.

"Good luck," she said.

"I won't let you down," I promised.

Then I flung the door open and left with my head held high, ready to get started on my mission.

I hope you loved The Vampire Wish series! If so, I'd love if you left a review. Reviews help new readers find the books, and I read each and every one of them :)

A review for the box set is the most helpful. Here's the link on Amazon ➜ The Vampire Wish Box Set

If you're not ready to leave the Vampire Wish world yet, I've written a novella about Jacen's first few days as a vampire that you can read for FREE! The novella starts when Jacen meets Queen Laila, and it's a story you don't want to miss.

To read Jacen's free novella, CLICK HERE or visit michellemadow.com/vampire-wish-novella.

While The Vampire Wish is over, the series continues with Noah and Raven's story in The Angel Trials!

Check out the cover and description for The Angel

Trials below. Then, keep reading for a sneak peek of the first few chapters! (You may have to turn the page to view the cover.)

She thought magic didn't exist. She was so, so wrong.

Raven Danvers is a typical student… until a demon attacks her on the night of her birthday. Luckily, she's saved by Noah—a mysterious, sexy wolf shifter who appears and disappears before she can ask him any questions.

Then Raven's mom is abducted by the same demon who

came after her. And who turns up at the scene of the crime again? Noah. He's hunting the demons who are taking humans, and he's ultimately heading where Raven needs to go to save her mom—the mystical island of Avalon.

Now Raven's joining Noah's demon hunting mission whether he wants her there or not. Which he doesn't. But nothing stops Raven, so she and Noah will have to learn to work together—if they don't kill each other first.

More importantly, she has to survive his crazy demon hunt. Because surviving is the only way to get to Avalon and save her mom's life.

Get your copy now at:
mybook.to/angeltrials

ABOUT THE AUTHOR

Michelle Madow is a USA Today bestselling author of fast paced fantasy novels that will leave you turning the pages wanting more! Her books are full of magic, adventure, romance, and twists you'll never see coming.

Click here or visit author.to/MichelleMadow to view a full list of Michelle's novels on Amazon.

To get free books, exclusive content, and instant updates from Michelle, visit www.michellemadow.com/subscribe and subscribe to her newsletter now!

THE VAMPIRE WAR

Published by Dreamscape Publishing

Copyright © 2017 Michelle Madow

ISBN: 1981581286
ISBN-13: 978-1981581283

❀ Created with Vellum

Made in the USA
Monee, IL
03 November 2020

46627334R00152